Vicki Blum

Wish Upon a Unicorn

Illustrated by

Alan Barnard

Scholastic Canada Ltd.

Toronto New York London Auckland Sydney
Mexico City New Delhi Hong Kong

Scholastic Canada Ltd.
175 Hillmount Road, Markham, Ontario, L6C 1Z7
Scholastic Inc.
555 Broadway, New York, NY 10012, USA
Scholastic Australia Pty Limited
PO Box 579, Gosford, NSW 2250, Australia
Scholastic New Zealand Limited
Private Bag 94407, Greenmount, Auckland, New Zealand
Scholastic Ltd.
Villiers House, Clarendon Avenue, Leamington Spa,
Warwickshire CV32 5PR, UK

Map by Paul Heersink/Paperglyphs.

Canadian Cataloguing in Publication Data

Blum, Vicki, 1955–
Wish upon a unicorn

ISBN 0-590-51519-5

I. Title.

PS8553.L86W57 1999   jC813'.54   C99-930551-4
PZ7.B6258Wi 1999

5 4 3 2   Printed and bound in Canada   9/9 0 1 2/0

*To the students and staff of
Good Shepherd School.*

. . . he hath as it were the strength of a unicorn.
Numbers 23:22

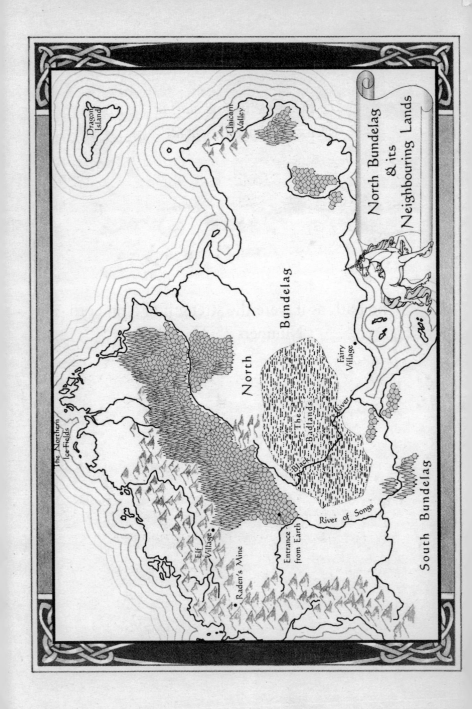

North Bundelag & its Neighbouring Lands

Dragon Island

Unicorn Valley

North Bundelag

The Northern Ice Fields

Fairy Village

The Black Badlands

River

Elf Village

Raden's Mine

Entrance from Earth

River of Songs

South Bundelag

Chapter 1

Arica's troubles all began when she fell through the crack in her grandmother's kitchen floor.

Though Arica loved her very much, she knew her grandmother was not the usual kind. Grandmother kept lizards in her bathroom sink. Wild plants hung from her ceiling in bunches. Strange bottles stood in rows on her pantry shelf. A painted stick and a cloak hung in her front hallway. And she had cracks in her floor big enough to fall through.

Arica fell for a very long time. She didn't remember the cellar being quite so far down. But then she had always seen the cellar as a good place to stay out of. It was too dark, and had odd damp smells and strange noises coming out of corners. The two times she had gone down, not very eagerly, were to get bottled peaches. But they weren't all the way in the back. They were kept close to the stairs because they were Grandmother's favourite and the reason for most trips to the cellar.

Arica landed with a thud on the hard, cold floor. The jolt rattled her teeth, took her breath entirely away and jarred every bone in her body. She lay where she fell, trying to gasp but not doing very well, and wondered how long it would take her to die from lack of air. Would it be long and painful, quick and easy, or somewhere in between?

That's when she noticed the trolls. Two of them had come out of nowhere and were standing over her. She wasn't sure how she knew what they were, since she'd never seen a troll in her life until this moment. But she could tell by their large, glowing red eyes; by their pale, warty skin; and, now that her breath was returning, by the terrible way they smelled. She tried to yell for help, but she was still too short on air to make a sound.

Not that it would have brought the help she needed, anyway. Grandmother was gone — this was the reason Arica was here watering plants in the first place. And the nearest neighbour was ninety-two years old.

"Ugly little thing, isn't she?" said one of the trolls.

He spoke in a language other than English, yet Arica understood every word.

"Yes," said the other, practically shuddering.

"But it's not her fault," the first admitted. "It's all that human blood running through her veins."

"Still, you have to agree she's frightful, even for a human," the second went on. "She has hair like a scrub mop and eyes with hardly any colour." He shivered. "She looks like a bundle of sticks put together with string. What do you want her for, anyway?"

"Never mind about that," said the first. "Pick her up and let's get going."

"I'll be worn out before we're halfway there," the second one whined. "I have a better idea. You take one end, I'll take the other."

At that point, Arica regained enough of her wits to start hitting and kicking for all she was worth. It didn't take her long to realize the trolls were much stronger and quicker than they looked. In a moment, a door in the farthest, darkest corner of the cellar opened with an eerie creak and Arica was plunged headlong into icy darkness.

By this time her breath had come back enough for her to begin to scream. But her opened mouth was quickly stuffed with an old, ratty handkerchief. Arica now found it so hard to breathe that she had to quit struggling or risk fainting dead away.

The trolls continued downward. It looked to Arica like they were taking her through some kind of long, underground tunnel.

She tried to remember if she'd ever heard Grandmother speak of her cellar, or what might lie under it, and came up with a blank. Well then, had her grandmother ever spoken of trolls? She couldn't recall any talk of them since she was a kid — and that had been only in stories.

Well, what about her parents? Father called Arica his "little princess" every now and then — mostly on birthdays. But that had nothing to do with trolls. (Besides, the title never really suited her, anyway. Princesses, at least the ones she'd heard of, didn't love sports, climbing trees and wearing faded blue jeans.)

And her mother? All Arica ever got from her were lectures on keeping her face and hands clean, being more tactful and getting her schoolwork done. Arica was absolutely, completely, bet-your-life-upon-it certain that her mother had never brought up the subject of trolls.

The tunnel ended suddenly. Arica and her captors spilled out at the base of a steep hill in the centre of a thickly wooded forest. Arica looked back, then stared in amazement as the cave opening blinked out of existence behind them, leaving only a blank wall of hill, trees and foliage.

She started to struggle anew and was rewarded with a sharp jab between the shoulder blades. By the time her back quit hurting, the ground had levelled off, and glimmers of light were beginning to peek through the darkness overhead. Soon the sky had grown bright enough for her to make out the branches of the surrounding trees and a pale sliver of moon.

A flock of birds drifted overhead, black blotches against the lightening sky. Their silhouettes sprinkled across the second moon's silver face.

The second moon? Arica looked back again, just to make sure. On one side of the sky was a slender arc of light; on the other a swollen, gleaming disk. Her heart thudded. No one she knew of had ever talked about a place with more than one moon.

Arica wished her father and mother had done a better job of warning her. They were good parents — she wasn't complaining about that. They often lectured her, with love and care, on not speaking to strangers and on getting home before dark. But when they had talked of all the dangers lying in wait for children who wandered off, they hadn't mentioned anything like this. They had led her to believe such places existed only in fairy tales!

The trolls dropped her so suddenly her face hit dirt. The rag was jarred from her mouth. She rolled, tasting mud and dead leaves. One of the trolls made a grab for her leg and missed. She could hear the other one grumbling, somewhere above and behind her.

"Come here, you filthy beast," the troll growled.

It took Arica a moment to realize the troll was not talking to her, but to someone or something else standing nearby. By the time she had figured this out and struggled to her knees for a better look, the troll had dragged the "filthy beast" close enough for her to see.

She stared up at the creature and gasped in dismay. A silver chain wound tightly around its neck, then ran down in a tangle through its mane and hung off one shoulder. The chain was so tight that in places the animal's flesh was chafed and reddened.

The "beast" was actually a horse.

Arica had always loved horses more than anything in the world. She drew them, read stories about them, and pasted pictures of them in scrapbooks. She'd even had lessons at a real riding school. Then there were the two weeks she'd spent at her uncle's ranch, chasing cows from one end of it to the other.

But Arica, in all her experience with horses, had never seen one so dazzlingly white in colour and so perfectly formed. Its mane and tail appeared not to hang but to float like silver clouds. Its legs were slender and shapely; its hooves were small and trim;

She stared up at the creature and gasped in dismay.

its fine neck was delicately arched.

Almost without thinking, Arica leaned toward the animal, reaching out with her hand. It turned its face toward her. The touch of its nose against her fingers was like an angel's kiss.

That's when she saw the horn.

It grew from the centre of the animal's forehead, like a stack of solid gold rings that started large and narrowed to a point. Then the unbelievable truth slowly dawned on Arica's groggy mind: this was what the storybooks called a unicorn.

Arica toppled backward in surprise, landing in a damp, slimy patch of forest moss. Before she could recover, a troll grabbed her by the shirt and yanked her upward. She twisted helplessly in his grasp. His harsh chuckles seemed to come from far away.

"Get over here and help me lift her," he growled to his companion. "We haven't got all night, you know!"

Arica felt herself being lifted high in the air, amid a series of groans and complaints from the trolls. The next moment, she was slung like a sack of prairie wheat over the unicorn's bare back. Lacking the strength to sit upright, she fell forward, her face burying itself in the animal's mane.

The trolls were now arguing about which direction to take, their words getting louder and angrier by the moment. Arica struggled to balance herself between the unicorn's shoulder blades so that she wouldn't slither to the ground at its first step.

The shouting rose to a peak, then abruptly ended. The next moment one of the trolls, whether in rage at his fellow or simply out of spite, yanked fiercely on the silver chain.

Arica could never have been prepared for what happened next. Perhaps it was because she loved horses so much. Or perhaps it was because of the cruel treatment she and the unicorn were being forced to endure, or maybe it was something else entirely.

As the chain tightened, digging into the animal's flesh, Arica felt a stab of pain go through her. It was the unicorn's pain: like fire and ice, like needles and knives, like a jolt of pure electric power.

And then the ground rose up to meet her.

Chapter 2

Arica came to her senses face down in a patch of wild rose bushes. At first she thought it had all been a bad dream. She felt cold and painfully stiff in the joints — probably, she thought, from having fallen out of bed.

Then she felt the bush's thorns pierce her skin, and she opened her eyes to the sight of two hooves attached to the ends of some very horsey-looking legs. She shifted her gaze upward. Sure enough, there was a chest, body, head and — no, it couldn't be — a golden horn.

She struggled up through the tangle, her head spinning. The unicorn stood motionless, one large brown eye fixed sadly upon her. She stared back, and felt a sudden urge to wrap her arms around its neck for whatever comfort and warmth she could get. She had an eerie feeling, from the way it looked at her, that this was the best friend she'd ever had — like she'd known the animal all her life. She shrugged the idea aside and turned warily toward the trolls.

The second moon was high overhead now and sent a splash of silver light down into the clearing where they stood. For the first time since she'd been taken, Arica was now able to get a good look at the trolls.

Troll One was the larger of the two, the one giving all the orders. He was about Arica's own height but at least twice as wide, with thick, heavy arms that dangled almost to his knees. Large red eyes, a beak-like, dirt-encrusted nose and a black-toothed slit of a mouth completed the distasteful picture. He was dressed like an eighteenth-century gentleman come upon hard times. He wore a tattered white shirt and a coat and breeches of blue satin, which might possibly have been clean at one time. His feet were large, hairy and bare.

Troll Two was smaller, dirtier and clad only in rags.

They were arguing again, about how to get Arica back up on the unicorn. Troll Two wanted to simply sling her aboard. Troll One's plan was to force the unicorn down on its knees.

Arica wasn't keen on any plan that might involve more pain for the unicorn. After managing to get up on two wobbly feet, she took one step toward the animal and toppled headfirst between its front legs. Troll Two's plan won out in the end, and Arica landed back on top of the unicorn with a heavy thump. The animal flinched. For the first time in her life, Arica felt glad that she was small and thin for her age.

She would have kicked the trolls in their ugly shins or stomped on their feet, right then and there, if she'd had the courage. She had never felt so helpless, not even when Ernie Elaschuk had pushed her and her new white sweater face-first into a mud puddle. But then Ernie Elaschuk was only an ordinary schoolyard bully. These trolls, she was beginning to discover, were playing a much more vicious game.

The sky was paling into dawn. Arica couldn't quite figure that one out. She'd only just fallen through her grandmother's kitchen floor, and it had been early evening then — hardly suppertime, as she recalled. Now, barely an hour later (by her guess), the moons were fading rapidly in a brightening sky.

Arica sighed and shrugged. After she figured out the unicorn, the two moons, the trolls (and why she understood everything the trolls said), she'd definitely look into this strange change in time.

It was now becoming easier to make sense of the direction they were taking. The trees had thinned and Arica could see what lay before them. The forest was dwindling into an expanse of grassy hill country, dotted with green shrubbery and splashed with flowers of red and mauve.

"Where are you taking me?" Arica asked, her voice squeaking in her own ears like a leaky balloon. She cleared her throat and repeated the question. She couldn't let the trolls know how frightened and alone she truly felt. They were the kind of creatures who would take advantage of any weakness.

But now they completely ignored her.

"Where are we going?" she repeated, trying to sound bold. "Answer me, if you don't mind."

"Nowhere that concerns you," Troll One snarled over his shoulder.

"I would think it does concern me, considering I'm going there," she snapped. But that was all she could manage. After a while she settled for chatting quietly to the unicorn. It at least had the courtesy to flick back an ear every now and then. She could have sworn that it understood her completely.

Arica heard the river before she actually saw it. She had always loved the sound of water, and had spent many happy hours on the riverside skipping rocks with her cousin Connor. But Arica had never heard anything like this. While the rivers of her homeland trickled, splashed, or roared along their way, this one played music. She could have sworn there were flutes, clarinets, saxophones — even a few French horns!

She soon realized that the sound was not actually a sound, but something that played deep inside her, like a song written in her soul. Her heart lifted, and sad feelings fell away. How could a place with rivers like this be all bad? She'd find a way out of this mess and back home again, that was for sure. And in the meantime, she'd make the best of a bad situation. She would watch and wait. Everyone had a weakness — even, she was certain, trolls.

A while later they paused at the riverbank for a drink. The trolls didn't offer to bring her down from her perch, so she clung to the unicorn's back while the trolls gulped and gurgled and the animal listlessly sipped. At last Troll Two thought to bring her some water he'd scooped into an old leather pouch. To Arica's surprise, he removed the ropes from her wrists so that she could drink. The pouch stank of old hair and sour milk, but the water was cold and sweet. It did for her body what the music had done for her spirits. She felt the tingle all the way to her toes.

After following the river for what seemed like several more hours, they changed direction and headed across country.

Arica glanced at her left wrist and for the first time noticed that it was bare. She'd lost her bracelet somewhere along the way, then. It had been a birthday gift from her mother and was made of real gold. It even had her name engraved on the back, and the date she was born. Her eyes watered and she rubbed at them angrily with her sleeve. There was no use asking the trolls to take her back. Even if they agreed (which she doubted), they had come too far through too much grass and forest undergrowth. She'd never find it now, even if she looked for a week.

The unicorn stopped so suddenly that Arica would have toppled between its ears had its head not jerked up at the same moment. As it was, she was flung against its neck with a knock that rattled her teeth. She pushed herself back up, coughing and spitting out strands of mane.

Troll Two let loose a string of words that Arica was sorry she understood. Then he readied to yank on the chain. But Troll One grabbed the other's arm and motioned frantically for silence.

They stood, not moving — hardly even breathing. Arica strained her ears for a sound, any sound. She wondered at the keenness of their hearing until she realized that it was the silence that had them scared — the complete silence. No twitter of insects greeted their ears. No chirping of birds. No scurrying of tiny feet through rustling grass.

The way Arica saw it, if all the animals in the area had gone into hiding, maybe it would be smart for them to do the same. Her father had always told her to pay attention to what animals did, because their senses were sharper than a human's.

She cleared her throat. "Don't you think we should — " she began. The next moment the ground exploded all around them.

A stream of tiny living things flew up from beneath their feet like a geyser. Then three things happened all at once. Arica dived off the unicorn's back; the unicorn reared, hooves flailing; and the trolls drew swords and yelled, "Pfipers!"

The creatures — tiny green snakes with wings — were faster than anything Arica had ever seen. They darted like hummingbirds. From their small green jaws flicked thin black tongues, and the rattling sound of their thousands of tails crawled up her spine like claws. She grabbed the only weapon she could find — a small stick lying on the ground — and began swinging with all her might.

The battle was hopeless from the start. The snakes bit as they flew — it wasn't long before Arica's arms and face were covered with tiny red punctures. She knew right away the creatures were poisonous as well, for already she'd begun to feel dizzy and heavy-limbed. Troll Two had sunk to the ground, too weak to remain on his feet. Troll One fared better — he was still taking swipes with his sword. The unicorn was shaking itself violently to keep the pfipers from landing on its back.

True One, something said inside Arica's head.

She whirled, knocking wildly at the flying pfipers.

Remove the chain, True One, the voice continued. *The silver . . . blocks the magic. You must touch my horn . . .*

The silver chain? Magic? A horn? Arica scrambled over the heap of fallen snakes on her way to the animal. She fumbled with the clasp, undid it at last and began to unwind the chain from around the unicorn's neck. Then, even as it rattled and fell free, the unicorn threw back its head. The next moment it pressed forward, touching the tip of Arica's stick with its horn.

Use the magic I have given you, True One, the creature said.

"I am small and not very brave," she said.

You are small, but brave enough, he replied.

Arica felt the stick grow warm against her palm. What she did next she did purely by instinct, without thought or plan. She raised her arms over her head with the stick held high in her hand, like a wizard's staff. It glowed in the early morning sunlight as she swept it around her head in one great wide arc.

There was a flash of blue, and then silence.

She raised her arms over her head with the stick held high in her hand . . .

The attacking pfipers lay still upon the ground. Troll One stood, shaken but alive. Troll Two pulled himself up, weak and dazed. The unicorn had disappeared and the silver chain lay in a heap of links where it had fallen. Arica gazed silently around her, then down at the stick in her hand. She watched numbly as it slipped from her fingers into a patch of weeds.

She stumbled backward and bumped into a rock. Then she slid weakly to her knees, put her face into her shaking hands and burst into tears.

Chapter 3

I'm still here, True One, said a voice inside Arica's mind.

Arica gulped down one last sob, ran her sleeve across her face and looked up. The unicorn was nowhere to be seen.

She did see Troll One, bending to pick up the silver chain. He stood there and scowled like it had somehow been the cause of all his troubles. Then he wound it around his middle like a gaudy belt.

"Where — " she started to say, sniffing again.

I am nearby. I will follow and watch. Rescue is not yet possible. When the silver chain is near, my magic and strength are gone.

"Don't go," Arica pleaded, but already the voice had left her, leaving her feeling strangely sorrowful and alone.

Troll One approached her, sword in hand. She drank from the offered pouch — warm water that tasted like dirty cat fur and curdled cream — and ate a few crumbs of dry biscuit he had dug from one of his back pockets.

The trolls kept to themselves while they ate, all the while muttering excitedly with their hunched backs to her face. Twice Troll Two glanced over his shoulder at her. Was it just her imagination, or did he actually look frightened? She tried to listen in but could only make out a few scattered phrases.

" . . . poison . . . much time . . . how far . . . " was all she heard. Then the two of them turned back, pulled her roughly to her feet and forced her to resume the trek.

Walking hurt Arica more than anything she could remember, except maybe the time she got her tonsils out. The bites on her face and arms had swelled and stung badly. Her head throbbed; her limbs felt like lead. The trolls were no better off, but at least they were stronger. And they weren't the ones being kidnapped and carted all over mountain, mead and marsh.

The endless walking was close to unbearable, but it gave Arica time to think. And thinking kept her mind off the pain she was in.

Her thoughts drifted. The memories that came to her were vague and wispy, like fading dreams. She thought of her mother's eyes, her hugs, her laughter, and then of all the rules she made that seemed so silly and unimportant. She remembered the times she thought of lying to her mother but couldn't — her mother saw through everything. She thought of the times she had wanted to run away. Now, if she ever got back home, she would never want to run away again.

She imagined playing soccer with Connor and winning. She remembered how it felt to climb into her own warm bed in her own safe room and have her father tuck her in.

She imagined him saying, "I love you, princess," and kissing her cheek. He would smell fresh and tangy, like the air after summer rain, like spices in old cupboards, like puppies scrubbed clean. She recalled that occasionally he seemed a little sad, like something wasn't quite right. He never told her why. At times she thought maybe he didn't know why, either. But it was always easy to make him smile again.

"I love you too, Father," she would say, throwing her arms around his neck. His cheek against her own would scratch and tickle till she pulled back giggling. When he left and turned out the light, she would no longer be afraid.

Then she thought about her grandmother.

The clues had been there all along, if she'd only been smart enough to read them. On those rare times when Grandmother came over for a visit, she never left without telling Arica a story. The tales were most often about elf children who had done something wrong and needed to learn a lesson. Arica had loved the stories when she was younger. They had seemed so vividly real. She could picture the elf children clearly in her mind, with their sad green eyes and their golden heads lowered in shame. Once in a while her grandmother even talked about fairies.

She had never mentioned trolls — but when Arica wanted to dress up as one a few Halloweens ago, it was the first time she ever saw the old lady angry. The way she figured it, looking back, was that Grandmother knew a lot more than she ever let on. Obviously she'd had some experience with trolls, or had at least heard what they were like and knew the danger. It was, after all, to her cellar that they had come.

Arica suddenly noticed that the flat grasslands had given way to a series of hills dotted with shrubs and trees. A string of jagged purple mountains loomed on the far horizon. Arica thought of escape, but couldn't figure out how she would ever be able to do it without the unicorn. Even if she could manage all on her own, where would she turn for help? She couldn't very well go around asking people if they'd seen her grandmother's cellar, with peaches in the front and a door in it leading to a world somewhere far away. Her best bet was to stick with these trolls, who definitely knew the way back. Somehow, some way, they must be persuaded to return her to where she belonged.

The next moment, a knife jabbed Arica's stomach.

It wasn't a real knife. It only felt like one. As she toppled to the ground, she cried out in pain. Then she lay curled up, gasping for breath.

Two blotched faces stared down at her. The trolls' glowing red eyes showed no concern, only mild interest.

"It's happening," one of them said.

"It won't be long for us, then," replied the other.

"What's happening?" Arica managed to ask between wheezes.

The trolls actually chose to answer her question, which told her something about the seriousness of the situation.

"The pfiper poison has a delayed effect," Troll One explained, with a fearful edge to his voice.

"Delayed effect!" Arica shrieked. "Nice of you to tell me!"

"Don't worry. If you survive the convulsions, you'll be fine."

The terrible part about it was that he wasn't even trying to be funny. Trolls, Arica decided, didn't know how to be funny.

After that the world seemed to disappear in a cloud of white-hot pain. A while later Arica became aware of something standing over her body. It had large nostrils that blew warm air into her face, gentle brown eyes and a horn growing out of the middle of its head. She had a feeling she had seen the creature before.

Don't be afraid, True One, it said. *I will help you.*

Then, just as in a dream, the horn touched her stomach, and the pain melted away as if it had never been.

Weariness hit her like a wave. Gratefully, she closed her eyes, but the creature wouldn't let her rest.

Climb upon my back, it said. *There is great danger. Others are coming.*

She knew she could trust the animal, even with her life. She reached for its neck to pull herself up, but the flood of tiredness was more than she could resist. She sank down into its blissful, blessed darkness.

Arica found herself in a dark dream world where she couldn't quite remember who she was. For a time she simply drifted, at rest in the black stillness. When she finally woke up, the first thing she saw was that she was surrounded by at least a dozen little men. They ran around in circles, jabbering in words she couldn't quite make out. She'd never seen men quite so ugly. Their heads were too big, their eyes bright and glowing and their arms dangled down past where arms should rightfully be. She wondered vaguely what they wanted as they grabbed her roughly and hoisted her up.

The world twirled like a top, and the pale faces melted into a swirling circle of white. Then Arica felt herself topple into the dirt.

She woke up — really woke up, this time — tied to a flat frame made of sticks that were joined to a pair of large tree branches. The whole affair, which looked a lot like a crude sled, was being pulled by two or three of the trolls' scruffy-looking horses. Arica couldn't actually see the trolls from where she lay, strapped down as she was beside Troll One, but there was no mistaking the sound of their complaining. Then she saw Troll Two's motionless body lying on the ground and it all came back with a jolt. Troll Two had not lived through the convulsions. Troll One, lying beside her, had barely survived.

So she was back to where she had started — a prisoner of the trolls. On the positive side, she was alive, and where there was life, there was hope. At least that's what she had always heard. At the moment she couldn't quite recall who had made that profound statement, or for what reason, but no matter, it worked for her. She'd bide her time and wait for the chance to get away. The only good thing about this whole situation was that it couldn't possibly get any worse. She slept.

The next time Arica opened her eyes it was dusk, and they had arrived at a prisoner-of-war camp.

At least that's what it looked like to Arica, going by the photographs she'd seen in books. Barbed-wire fences circled a large area of bare, packed dirt. In the centre huddled a clump of dirty, decrepit buildings. Troll guards stood post every few dozen metres. Dogs barked. A cold wind moaned.

A pathway from the compound led to the base of a dark, ragged mountain. From a gaping hole in the rock spilled men and women — all of them very small, dirty, pale and thin. They were bound together in one long line, with ropes.

If Arica hadn't been so tired and weak from lack of food, she would have made a dash for freedom right then and there. Instead all she could do was stare, as the gate to the prison rattled open to admit their little group.

As soon as they entered the compound Arica was shocked again. For there, in one corner of the enclosure, was a pen. Inside the pen, chained in silver to posts, were half a dozen unicorns. Their hides shone pale in the fading light. Their dark, knowing eyes gazed wearily at her from the shadows. Patches of reddened skin stood out on their coats.

"No," Arica whispered. She could feel their pain inside her, like an ache.

At last, a voice sounded in her mind. *You have come.*

One of the trolls cut the ropes that were holding her down. She sat up so suddenly that little lights danced in front of her eyes. "The trolls have hurt you," she said to the unicorns. "Why are they doing this?"

It doesn't matter, now that you are here.

Without thinking, she reached out her hand toward them. Then she looked up and saw her own father standing above her.

This second shock lasted for a few heart-throbbing seconds, until she realized this man was not really her father after all. He did look a lot like her father, she had to admit, but there were major differences. Both men were tall and dark, with thin eyebrows, narrow noses and dark eyes. But the man who stood before Arica now was older and heavier than her father. Arica's father's eyes were not so cold, his jaw line not nearly as severe. And his brow could never be so furrowed with hate.

The man who was clearly not Arica's father gazed down at her with scorn.

Then he seemed to recognize something in her, as well, and his look of disdain changed to surprise. His eyes widened as Arica stared defiantly back at him. She could hear the air hissing through his teeth.

"A human!" he growled. "You fools! What have you done? Don't you realize humans are nothing but trouble?"

"We know, Lord Raden," growled one of the trolls resentfully, "but we couldn't very well leave her to die. We found her in the forest, suffering from the effects of pfiper poisoning. On the ground some distance away we found two trolls who had also been bitten. One of them was still alive." He gestured at Troll One, still silent on his bed.

"Od! Ah, yes." The man paused and rubbed his brow, as if to relieve a nagging pain. Then he continued, "I knew he was up to no good. But this is just too stupid, even for him."

He turned from them all with a wave of his hand.

"Bring Od to me when he wakes. Throw the human girl in with the elves. See how much work you can get out of her before she collapses. She won't last out the week, I'm sure."

Then he walked away without a backward glance.

Chapter 4

The building Arica was taken to had rough wooden walls, a dirt floor and at least a hundred rickety bunks lined up in rows. Each one was covered with a woven-grass mat and a thin brown blanket. There were no pillows to be seen.

The few existing windows were small, high up and covered with iron bars. Most had cracked or broken glass. The air in the room was cold and damp, and smelled of smoke and mouldy cheese.

It looked as if meals were cooked and eaten in the same place. At one end of the room, a large tabletop was supported by the sawed-off trunks of four trees. Arica approached hopefully, but found that the meal was as dismal as the surroundings. Lumpy grey gruel was being served in bowls, along with chunks of dark bread and what looked like leftover dishwater in cups.

She sat on one of the bunks with a cup in one hand and a bowl in the other, surrounded by workers. None of them looked at her or spoke.

The mush stuck in her throat like glue and the bitterness of the bread brought tears to her eyes, but her hunger forced her to finish every bite. When the pain in her stomach was almost gone, she began to stare around the room.

The workers were even dirtier and thinner up close. They were made up of the very young, the very old and every age in between. They all had the same yellow-gold hair, ears that ended in points and large, long-lashed green eyes. None of them was any taller than she was.

These were the elves of her grandmother's stories.

It was the children who made her throat ache and her heart feel like it would swell and burst within her chest. She wasn't surprised that they were thin, dirty and ragged, and clung to their mothers' skirts begging for food. What surprised her most was the fact that they didn't cry or complain — not even when they were turned away, still hungry. Then she saw the hopeless looks on their tiny pale faces.

Arica returned her empty bowl and cup to the

table as she saw the elves doing, washed them in a tub of grey, greasy water and hung them on pegs to dry.

She walked up to the nearest elf — who happened to be one of the older ones.

"Hello," she said, smiling and holding out her hand. "My name is Arica. What's yours?"

The elf stared down at the offered hand. Her eyes filled with pity. Arica felt fingertips, dry and hard as bones, brush against her own.

"You poor child," the old woman said in a voice that rasped like a rusty hinge. "What will become of you? Where will the fairy Raden throw you when he is done?" Then she turned her face away, coughed wretchedly into an old cloth and shuffled past. Arica stared at her — the stooped shoulders, the dull tattered dress that hung like a sack, the ragbag sweater covering it all — and wondered what would become of all of them.

She looked around. None of the others paid her any attention. In fact, they seemed to be going out of their way to avoid her. With a sigh and a shrug, she returned to her bunk, pulled the one thin blanket up over her ears and fell asleep.

She dreamed of home. In her dream the whole family had gathered for Sunday dinner. Her father and mother were there, of course, and her grandmother.

But what most surprised her was the presence of her grandfather, who'd passed away when Arica was four years old.

She could see him as clearly as if she were standing next to him. Curly grey hair erupted above a rosy, round face and twinkling blue eyes. A beard to match sprang from his chin in every possible direction. Hands that could twist iron playfully tossed her into the air, then caught her coming down. Arica laughed and wrapped her arms as far as she could around his portly middle.

Then her grandfather held her at arm's length and looked deep into her eyes.

"Arica," the old man said. His voice was strangely quiet and he was no longer smiling. "You are a very special girl, and only you can do what must be done. Don't ever give up. You are much stronger than you think. You are much braver than you think."

Her dreaming self knew her grandfather had made a mistake, and wondered how she would ever tell him.

Later Arica woke up to the sound of a terrible clatter, her grandfather's last whisper still drifting through her mind. A troll stood in the doorway with iron pots in both hands. He banged them together again and again — for effect, Arica supposed, since no one in the room could possibly have slept through the first clash.

Through a dirty window Arica could see that dawn had come to this dreary place. She rose with the elves and breakfasted on dry crusts and lumpy, sour milk. Then she was bound to the elves with ropes and led to the mine.

Arica had never been in a mine before. She'd learned all about them in school, and had even seen them in pictures. She remembered hearing on the news one time of a mine that caved in, killing a lot of men. She'd heard that in England, over a century ago, people had used children to work in the mines and had paid them hardly anything at all. But that had been given up long ago as uncivilized. These mines were sure to be better than the ones in old England.

After the first few hours she knew she was wrong. Nothing in England could have been as bad as this. The darkness she could have put up with, or the wetness, or the cold, but not all three of them at once for so long a time. What little light they had — buckets of burning coal scattered here and there, as well as tiny fire-lamps attached to their helmets — flickered and stank. It gave her head a pounding ache that wouldn't go away, even when she closed her eyes.

But all of this was nothing compared to the agony

she felt coming from the minds of the unicorns.

After the first hour she knew exactly what was expected of her. It was all quite simple, really. Explosives were set off, and when the dust cleared she and the elves went in with pickaxes and shovels. Raw ore was loaded into carts which were hitched to the unicorns. The animals then dragged the impossibly heavy loads upward and outside.

Arica realized that it wasn't the backbreaking toil or the cruel harnesses that were hurting the unicorns so much, but the place itself. She knew, without knowing how or why, that these animals were creatures of warmth and light and freedom. If they were kept away from those things too long, they would die.

It was beyond Arica why the trolls were using unicorns in the first place. Wasn't there a mule or a pack horse to be found in the neighbourhood? The trolls had brought her here with horses, hadn't they? The way she saw it, there had to be a good reason for using the less hardy unicorns. The man who she had thought was her father, and who was clearly in charge here, couldn't possibly be as foolish as he was mean.

By the time they headed back down the hill that evening, Arica was beyond caring about anything but sleep. After a few hasty slurps of gruel and a gulp or two of water that tasted like it was poured from an old boot, she fell upon the mat, too worn out to even pull the blanket up over her legs.

Later, through a tired haze, she heard voices and felt someone cleaning her face and hands with a wet cloth.

"Mother?" she moaned, trying to open her eyes.

"What do you know," said a harsh male voice somewhere nearby. "Humans have mothers after all."

"You're being unkind, Perye," replied the voice of a girl. "All humans aren't bad. They're just like the rest of us — some good, some not so good, some in between."

"Bah — they're all thieves," growled the boy elf. "They took our land, stole our food, enslaved our people for their magic. Their ancestors drove our ancestors into the North when we dared to fight back. Now their cities pollute the warm southern lands where we used to live."

"All those things happened hundreds of years ago. You said it yourself, Brother: it was our ancestors and hers, not you and her." The girl gently pushed a lock of hair off Arica's brow. Arica tried to speak but could only produce a small groan.

"The fight isn't over yet, Drusa," Perye insisted. "We're still recovering from what we lost in the Great War. When I think of the magic we once had . . ." His bitter words ground to a halt.

"How could I forget," she said, "when we're told about it from childhood? It's true that humans have treated us badly in the past. But you're leaving out the good part on purpose."

"Oh? There's a good part?"

"The part of the story that tells how someday a fairy with great powers will come and unite our two countries. Then the lost fairies will return, magic will be kept from disappearing from the land, and everyone will live in peace and happiness."

Perye's laughter sounded like hail on an old tin roof.

"Do you really swallow all of that?" he said. "If you do, then you're dumber than I thought."

She sighed. "Maybe that's our whole problem. We've stopped believing in the old prophecies. We blame everybody else for our problems."

"Now what is that supposed to mean?"

"Well, you don't see many humans in North Bundelag, do you? But we elves are still at odds with each other. You know how it is. We all think our village is the best, our children are the brightest, our ways are the only right ones. Here we are in this terrible place, with an elf village only a day away, and our own people have done nothing to help us. Not to mention all the fighting we do with the trolls. Whose fault is that, Perye?"

Hearing this, it occurred to Arica that fighting

trolls was not such a bad idea. She would have said so, and boldly, too, but it was too late. She had lost the battle to stay awake.

The next morning she wondered if she'd dreamed the entire episode, it was so vague and sketchy in her mind.

The elves ignored her as completely as ever, and her second day in the mine was as miserable as the first. At mealtime that night (if you could call mouldy biscuits and a meat paste that tasted like dog food a meal), she overheard one of the elves calling Perye by name. She quickly looked up to see which elf he was.

Perye's gaze fell upon Arica and their eyes met and held. For one brief moment the elf's anger toward her and her kind flared in his eyes like a silent green flame. Then Arica knew it had been no dream.

Chapter 5

By the fourth day Arica had overheard enough bits of conversation to get an idea of where she was.

She had been brought to a land made up of two countries — North and South Bundelag. North Bundelag, the country that was somehow attached to Grandmother's cellar, was the smaller of the two, with ice fields in the north and areas of farmland and forest throughout. Somewhere in the middle was a wasteland, mentioned once or twice but never talked about at length. There were no cities, but many small towns and villages dotted the country-side.

Nothing modern existed here and the people

(made up mostly of elves and trolls) drove carts, grew their own food and believed in magic. Not only did they believe, but they also practised it as part of their everyday life. They all had some ability in the use of magic — though fairies and unicorns were by far the most powerful. But unicorns were scarce and kept to themselves, and all but a few of the fairies had disappeared during the Great War that Perye had spoken of. It was feared that if things kept on the way they were going, the art of magic might soon be lost forever.

There was one in the land who still had great magic, however. She was the Fairy Queen who ruled North Bundelag, and she lived in a fairy village on the East Coast.

South Bundelag, by comparison, was large, wealthy and populated mostly by humans. It had cities, factories and even some advanced technology. The elves spoke of wagons that produced noise and great clouds of steam (trains, perhaps). They mentioned iron sticks that barked and killed from a distance (obviously guns) and light without fire (could it possibly be electricity?). Magic was something the people of South Bundelag didn't take too seriously, yet would gladly use if they could get it.

But at the present time South Bundelag was far more interested in gold, silver and copper than in magic. It seemed the South was a bit short of these metals, and was desperate to get hold of as much of them as it could. Certain people in South Bundelag (namely a few of the rich merchants who ran the country) felt it was their right to just come into North Bundelag and take whatever they wanted.

Arica was no expert on politics, but spears and swords against an army triple its size didn't give the North, in her opinion, a ghost of a chance. So far the Fairy Queen had managed to prevent a takeover by sheer hard work, fast talking and — the elves suspected — a little magic. Her toughest job, however, was trying to get the trolls to join in with them. Trolls were known for refusing to take sides unless there was some kind of profit to be made. They had no loyalty — not to home, friends nor even family. And they didn't care the least about who was in power so long as they were left to do as they pleased. Elves, on the other hand (according to themselves, anyway), were loyal and trustworthy and would fight to the death for their families and their country.

Meanwhile, someone was running an illegal operation, doing secret business with the South, and getting very rich in the process. That someone was Raden.

Raden was in revolt against the laws of his own land. He was enslaving its citizens and putting them to work in his mine. And the Fairy Queen, so busy with all the talking, the travelling, the keeping of peace within and keeping the enemy out, either didn't know about it yet or hadn't figured out how to stop it.

Arica had landed right in the middle of it all.

She had also, by watching carefully, learned a great deal about the operation of the mine.

The raw ore the elves chipped out of the mountain was hauled by cart and unicorn to a large brick furnace not too far from the mouth of the mine. There it was melted down under very high heat. The sight and feel of all that fire looked downright dangerous — enough to deter any child from playing with matches.

Once the metal was cooled it was stuffed into bags and locked in a shed until more trolls arrived on horseback (not unicorn-back, Arica noted) to take them away.

It was plain as the hairs on a troll's chin that the mine's output was large. And because of the free — to be frank, slave — labour provided by the elves and unicorns, Raden was likely making a very tidy profit.

By mid-afternoon of the fourth day Arica was no longer feeling like each day here might be her last — although she was still so tired she could hardly think. She couldn't help but compare this to the soccer season at home. The first few days of practice made her so stiff and sore she could hardly get up in the morning, but by the third or fourth day she would start to toughen up. This was what was happening here. Somehow, instead of wasting away, she was toughening up.

As she enjoyed this pleasant thought, the roof of the mine caved in upon her.

What really happened, Arica later learned, was that a small earthquake took place, making the rocks shift upward from below. This put pressure on the walls and ceiling of the mine, forcing them to go places and do things they were never meant to do.

As the rocks started heaving and flying, Arica fell, then rolled against a wall. Through a haze she saw a mass of stones rain down upon Perye, who had been working near her. The two unicorns who had been working with them were luckier. Even before the first tremor, the foal had scrambled to its mother, pressing itself against her side. Both foal and mother came through nearly untouched.

When the quake finally ended, Arica found herself bruised and cut, but alive. Perye was nowhere in sight.

The first thing Arica did was dive for the place she'd last seen the elf. She grabbed at rocks with her bare hands and flung them aside. Fortunately she didn't have far to dig, and in a matter of minutes she found Perye. A fist-sized lump bulged from his left temple.

Arica felt for a pulse and found one, weak but still fluttering. Carefully, she lowered her head to his chest and listened for the sound of breathing. She heard one gasp, and another, then nothing.

"No," she sobbed. She stared down at her own shaking hands, and at the elf's pale face against the dark rock, and tried to remember what must be done. She had to blow into his mouth. Yes, that was it. She had to try to breathe for him.

True One, said a calm voice inside her, breaking through the panic. *Use my foal's magic to heal the elf. Her power is not blocked by the silver, for she is unchained.*

Arica looked up at the mother unicorn, startled. She remembered . . . something about pfiper poison, another unicorn, and a touch that had taken away her pain.

She became aware of the light that flowed from the foal's tiny horn. It filled the dark mine and allowed her to see. The foal looked at her shyly, pranced in a little circle and leaped over a rock. Then it flicked its tail right under her nose, ducked behind its mother and peered out at Arica with two bright eyes from beneath her belly.

Tell her to come, True One, said the voice.

"I don't know how," she managed to rasp out. "And why do you unicorns keep calling me that?"

Summon her by name.

Arica opened her mouth in protest. How was she supposed to know its name without being told?

The next instant she knew.

It came to her in a flash. It was like a math problem you can't quite solve so you go back to it later and suddenly the answer is there, and you can't figure out how you could possibly have not known in the first place.

"Wish," Arica said, addressing the foal by name. "Come to me, Wish."

Wish popped out from behind her mother. She bounced around a pile of rubble, tossed her head three times, whinnied, then danced a sidestep over to where Arica sat with Perye's head cradled in her arms. She stood gazing at Arica for one long moment, then lowered her head and placed the tip of her horn directly on the lump.

Arica felt the power. It tingled through the entire length of her body, raising the hair on her arms and legs and warming her insides.

What she saw was even more spectacular.

The white light from Wish's horn dimmed and a paler blue light — exactly like the one Arica had seen in her battle with the pfipers — left the tip of her horn and flowed over the elf. It started at his head, then moved downward until his entire body was awash in blue. Right before Arica's eyes, the elf twitched and sucked in one great, ragged breath of

. . . a paler blue light . . . left the tip of her horn and flowed over the elf.

air. Then the lump faded and was gone.

It was over. Wish lifted her head, took a few backward steps, then sprang into the air and pranced over to her mother.

"Thank you, Wish," Arica managed to whisper.

Perye stirred. Arica looked into the elf's eyes — eyes that gazed up at her without seeming to know who she was. Then they fell shut, and Perye slept. Arica could see that where the horn had touched the lump it had left behind a red welt about the size of a dime.

By Arica's guess, it was less than an hour later when she heard the first faint cry coming from behind the wall of rock. By then the light cast by Wish's horn was almost gone — either the foal had used up too much magic in the healing or she was simply conserving energy. It was growing awfully dark and unbearably cold, so Arica yelled back — sleeping elf or no sleeping elf.

It took another hour or more for their rescuers to break all the way through. Arica helped from her side as best she could but found that her stiff and aching hands could hardly grip the stones.

At last, the gap in the rubble widened enough to let in one troll, then another, then many. Arica jumped in surprise when she suddenly came face to face with Troll One — Od. She pulled back from him in dismay. A large purple bruise marked the left side of his face. His lips were swollen and cut. One plainly did not betray Raden and get off easily. Arica almost felt sorry for Od, until she saw the look of evil in his eyes. Obviously, he blamed her for the state he was in. Her heart thudded with fear.

But her attention was then drawn to Drusa, who was crawling in through the jagged hole, a torch in her hand. When Drusa's gaze fell upon Perye, she rushed over to his side.

She remained there for so long without moving that Arica worried for a moment that Perye had stopped breathing again. But as Arica drew closer she saw that Drusa's already-pale skin had gone even whiter.

The girl elf was staring, with wide-eyed shock, at the tiny red welt.

Chapter 6

"Unicorns are holy animals," Perye explained. "Even here, where they are chained and imprisoned, we don't touch them. It would show a lack of respect."

Arica and Perye were sitting on the ground outside of the mine. Mounds of rubble lay at their feet. Elves and trolls toiled with overflowing wagons. Wounded mine workers were being tended by Drusa and others. Raden moved among them like a black cloud, snarling, snapping orders and kicking anything that got in his way.

Arica was too tired and sick to move. She sat and shivered with her back to a rock, wrapped in tattered quilts.

"But you didn't touch the unicorn," Arica protested. "She touched you."

Perye shook his head. "I know that. But the baby unicorn is pure and untainted, a creature of light and wind and magic. The rest of us — well, let's say we belong to the earth. We're sort of stuck down here, knee-deep in the muck. Do you know what I mean? They're different. They deserve better."

"They would probably say we all deserve better," said Arica. "Has anyone ever asked them what they think, or how they are feeling?"

"Asked them?" Perye looked at her blankly, like she'd just sprouted wings from her shoulders and a tail out behind.

"Yes, asked them."

"No one talks to unicorns," he stated flatly. "They say it's possible if you are chosen, but that's only hearsay. It's never happened that I know of."

At that point Arica decided not to tell him about the unicorns talking in her head. She could tell by the look on his face he wouldn't believe her. Besides, he actually seemed to be starting to like her. If she tried to put a wild tale like that one past him, he'd be back to treating her like something he'd dug up from the bottom of a trash bucket.

But she wasn't finished with him. "When I was coming here, there was a unicorn with us. He was the first unicorn I had ever seen. He saved our lives."

Perye looked doubtful. "That rarely happens. They usually keep to themselves."

"He was a prisoner like the ones here."

Perye's eyes suddenly flared green with anger. "Someday Raden will pay for what he has done."

"Look," Perye said, sighing impatiently. "I've studied unicorns and magic all my life. And I know this: unicorns have great magic, and they befriend no one. Why do you think Raden hates them so much? Because they withhold their power from him. If they can't be used, he wants them all destroyed, and their magic with them. But first he lets the trolls do his dirty work against them, so they suffer."

"And Raden gets rich in the process," Arica added under her breath.

Perye smiled wryly. "Yes. If nothing else, he's practical."

"Do you still hate me?" Arica asked, suddenly needing to know. "Have you changed your mind about me, and about humans?"

The elf looked her square in the face, more puzzled than angry. "I don't know," he said. "I'm not sure what happened in there. I still don't believe it. But it's clear you helped to save my life. For that, I'm grateful. I'll put it this way: perhaps there is one good human, after all."

"Well, it's about time!" exclaimed a voice behind them. They turned to see Drusa's smiling face.

"This is progress," the elf girl said, winking at Arica.

"He still has a long way to go, but it's a start!"

Arica felt a great burden suddenly lift from her shoulders. For the first time since arriving in this dreadful place, she had someone she could almost call a friend. She was no longer alone.

"I have two more questions," she managed to say, swallowing hard at the lump in her throat. "The first is, where did the humans in your world come from?"

Perye and Drusa looked at each other. The silence dragged painfully. Finally, Perye answered.

"From yours," he said reluctantly. "There was a terrible disease. Your people were dying. Then the cracks were discovered and many fled here, seeking refuge."

"Cracks?"

"Openings between your world and ours."

"What happened in the Great War?" Arica wanted to know. "What became of the fairies?"

"That makes three questions," Drusa said, grinning. But she answered. "A couple of hundred years later things fell apart. Your people started to use us all, for free labour and for our magic. There was a lot of fighting, and many elves — and trolls, unicorns and fairies — were killed."

Perye scowled. "Almost half of us died, but more trolls survived. They decided the risk was too great and took to the North long before the fighting was over. The war used up all the magic in us. It has taken generations to regain what little we are capable of today. But the elves managed to take thousands of humans down with them as they fell."

"And the fairies?"

Here Drusa took up the tale again. "The cracks had to be closed to stop the people of your world from coming to ours. The only way to do it was from your side. Thousands of fairies were needed. Their strength and magic were so depleted by the battles that it took many, working together, to close each crack. Once this was done, the fairies were to make their way, in your world, to the one remaining crack, which would be carefully guarded until all the fairies had returned. But most never made it. Too much time spent on your side erased their memories of who they were and where they came from. They were left behind, lost in your world."

"If fairies can live in my world without being discovered," Arica concluded, "then there must not be much difference between humans and fairies in how they look. Raden certainly looks like an ordinary grown-up to me."

Perye hesitated, then cleared his throat. "I've been told that the humans who first came to Bundelag were dirty and uncivilized. They were easy to distinguish from fairies then. Nowadays the differences aren't as clear. The best way to tell a fairy from a human is to see a fairy work magic. Fairies have great skill in magic, whereas a human couldn't call up fire to a pile of dry twigs. Another big difference is that fairies live longer, and don't actually die."

"You mean they live forever?" Arica gasped.

"No, they cease to exist like everyone else," Perye said. "What I mean is, they don't die in the same way we do. They don't stop breathing, get cold and rot like old leaves. I've never actually seen it happen, of course, but it's common knowledge: fairies simply fade away."

"Fade away?"

"Yes. Their bodies get more and more transparent, I've heard, until you can start to see through the thinner parts of them, like their fingers and toes. Then you see through all of them, and in the end they just disappear."

"It sounds terrible," said Arica, shuddering.

"Look at it this way. It's clean, if nothing else. And the biggest advantage is that nobody has to bury the body."

Arica never discovered if he was kidding or not, for the next moment they were interrupted by an uproar near the entrance to the mine. Perye tried to get up, but sank back with a groan. Arica struggled to stand, clutching her blankets, and made her way closer to the commotion. Trolls were shoving and shouting.

From where she stood, Arica could see that a large male unicorn had somehow come free of his chains and was zapping trolls left and right. They leaped and dashed wildly about, trying to avoid the bolts of flame that streamed from the tip of the animal's golden horn.

The creature reared, hooves slashing, the air snapping with uncontrolled magic. Arica literally felt the hair rise from her scalp and fingers of energy tickle her spine. Then she felt the unicorn's anger like a blow and fell to her knees. At the same moment, she realized who he was.

This unicorn hadn't come from the mine at all. He had followed her, watching and waiting for a chance to free her, just as he had promised.

"Light," she said, calling him by name, her head pounding with pain. "This is not a good time. There are too many of them."

She stopped, realizing that the animal could not possibly hear her — not from this distance, through all that racket. And she'd barely whispered the words.

There will never be a good time, came the reply inside her head.

Arica stood.

Rocks exploded at Light's feet; dust flew. It looked like a fireworks show, only the sparks were going down instead of up.

The next moment, Raden reached the unicorn. He paused, his eyes dark with rage and his face twisted and ghastly under the glaring sun. A large black stone glittered in the palm of his right hand. Arica could feel the air grow thick and heavy with gathering power.

"A soothstone," Drusa gasped, coming up beside Arica. "How dare he!"

The stone was old, rough-edged and pitted. It looked like Raden had dug it up from the very centre of the earth. The feeling Arica got from it was one of unspeakable evil.

"What is a soothstone?" she whispered to Drusa, knowing it couldn't be good.

"They're commonly used for telling the future," Drusa whispered back, her eyes fearful. "They come from deep underground and have the magic of the earth in them. Usually they're harmless — neutral, rather — but a large one like this, in the hands of a fairy like Raden, can draw up more bad magic than I care to think about."

Raden pointed the stone directly at the unicorn.

"Take cover!" Drusa hissed, and ran.

A bolt of red light flew from the stone. In an instant it was met by the clear blue flame that spewed forth from the unicorn's forehead. Waves of red and blue fire rolled together into a swirling storm of power. Tree branches snapped. Wind howled.

Arica stood, frozen in place, as the red flame moved slowly but steadily closer to the unicorn, devouring the blue light.

Light would die, and she could not allow it. She knew now that she was a chosen one. She was tied to them in a bond she could not understand or explain.

What she did next, she did without thinking or planning. When the red fire reached the tip of the unicorn's horn, and the blue light was almost gone, Arica threw herself, chest first, directly into the ugly red flame.

She fell to the ground, feeling nothing, unable to move. The red flame was gone. Light had fallen to the ground, weak and fighting for breath, but alive. And Raden stood looking down at her.

Out of the corner of her eye Arica could see a lot of trolls shouting and rushing about. They were gathered around the fallen unicorn. One of them was holding up an armful of silver chains.

Some of them came over to her and started grabbing at her, but they were shooed away by Raden. He gazed down at her with hostility touched with — could it be? — respect.

Raden put the stone back into his pocket, squatted down beside Arica and laughed. It was a harsh, heavy sound, without humour or warmth.

"You are much more than you seem, little human

girl," he said. "Tell me, who are you? Who are your parents?"

"I'd rather not say," Arica replied, glaring up at him. She would trust this man when the sunny Sahara froze over.

"Are your parents named Warman?" he asked. His cold, grey eyes gleamed.

She remained silent.

"It's funny what can happen to friends of girls who don't cooperate," growled the fairy, glancing toward Drusa and Perye.

"Yes," Arica said through clenched teeth.

"As I thought," Raden said with satisfaction, rising to his feet. "Od, fool that he was, reached into your world and brought you here without any idea of what he was doing. No matter. I will turn this to my advantage."

He spoke to the trolls. "Throw the girl into the pit. When her strength comes back, bring her to me."

Gesturing toward the elves, he added: "Make them clean up the mess and then send them back to the mine. If they can stand on two feet, they're fit."

Arica would have kicked him — had she been able to move.

Chapter 7

The pit was a huge hole dug into the ground. It was covered by a grate made of tree branches that let in air, but not much light. Dry grass and leaves were strewn across its bare dirt floor. Its walls were damp and loose, and roots curled out of them like a hundred tiny snakes. Arica lay shivering, too weak to pull the thin blanket up over her shoulders.

Outside, daylight went and came and went again. Water and soupy gruel was lowered down to her by rope, morning and night. Arica slept deeply and slowly grew stronger.

Once she woke up thrashing and calling for her mother after being chased by Trolls One and Two through a maze of black halls and tumbling rock.

On the third morning she opened her eyes to a shaft of sunlight upon her face and a voice like bells tinkling in her head.

True Arica, it said.

"Wish," she whispered, sitting up so suddenly the walls tilted around her. "Where are you, Wish?" From overhead came the sounds of tapping feet and snorting. Dust and dead leaves drifted down from above.

Arica True want, said Wish.

"I love you too, Wish," she said. "What have you been doing all this time?"

Wait.

"Waiting for me?" Arica asked. "I'm so glad some-body cares."

Care, said Wish.

"Do you have any idea how to get me out of here?"

Arica heard a snort, and hoof sounds that grew distant, then faded altogether. She sighed.

Arica stood up, and felt no pain other than a slight throbbing behind her eyes. Not bad for what she'd been through these past few days. She walked a circle around the pit — it took about three sec-onds.

Well, she said to herself. What now?

As it turned out, the news of her recovery trav-elled quickly. About a half-hour later the grate was flung aside, daylight blazed in from above, and one end of a rope landed in her lap.

Od the troll hauled her up. He scowled at her a moment, not speaking, then led her to a small building set apart from all the others. There she found an old tin tub filled to the brim with warm, soapy water.

As she soaked, she vowed never again to take bathtubs or hot running water for granted.

When her white, shrivelled skin had almost come clean, and she'd scrubbed her hair three times, she dried herself and put on the clothes Od had brought. She followed him into the next room, where Raden sat calmly waiting in a wood-and-animal-skin chair.

The room itself nearly took Arica's breath away. It was grand, in its own rugged way — but that wasn't it. What set her heart to pounding was that it was filled with things that were clearly not from Bundelag. They were from Arica's world.

The mounted head of a lion hung on one wall. A bald eagle with a rabbit in its claws rested upon a wooden table. A rug made from the hides of several Arctic foxes covered the floor between them. Trophies sprouted from walls, spilled over furniture, spread across floors. Some of the animals she recognized, but others she didn't.

Raden smiled at her and gestured for her to sit.

Arica perched carefully on the edge of a stool, unable to tear her eyes from the amazing collection.

"You stole these animals from my world," she said finally, swallowing painfully.

"Only some of them," Raden replied. He touched his fingertips together and gazed out over them. "Fascinating place, where you come from. Incredible variety of wildlife. Could never live there, though. Magic is scarce. And your cities! It's like walking through an explosion of light and noise. Don't humans ever sleep?"

Arica's stomach lurched. "You know the way back, then?"

"Homesick, are you?" He laughed, his eyes filled with glee. He clearly enjoyed seeing her suffer. "Forget the place. It's not worth it. Join me here, and together we'll rule the world."

Arica could hardly believe what she had just heard. What did Raden need her for? She was a girl — still a kid — not yet able to get a real job or drive a car, and here he was offering her half a world. Something didn't add up. She may have been young, but she wouldn't let herself be tricked.

"Why do you want me to help you?" she said. "I'm only a kid."

"Ah. You don't know, then."

"Know what?"

"Who you really are and where you come from. The soothlight would have burned a hole right through a mere human. But not you, my not-so-human girl. You're much more than you seem."

Arica felt like all her air had suddenly been cut off. Her heart pounded in her throat.

"My parents are Michael and Lynn Warman," she said doggedly, trying to keep a grip on reality. "They live in Calgary, Alberta, Canada. They are totally human. I go to school with four hundred other totally-human kids. That is, I did until a week ago, when I fell through the crack in my grandmother's kitchen floor."

"You didn't fall. Od collected you. I'm not sure how he managed it," Raden's eyes narrowed, "but he pulled you through the crack. Fool. He thought he was powerful because he knew my secret. But his power is only an illusion. He has no idea who he has brought me."

Arica leaped to her feet, her arms flailing. One hand struck the stuffed eagle and sent it skittering across the table. Raden jumped forward just in time to keep it from crashing to the floor.

His eyes blazed at Arica with anger and loathing. "You little fool," he hissed in a voice more terrifying than a shout. "What are you doing?"

"You have no right to keep me here!" Arica howled. "Let me go home! I didn't want to come here in the first place. It's not fair to take someone when they don't want to go! My mother is going to cry — and my father will be very, very angry! I hate it here! I hate your stupid mine and your ugly trolls, but I especially hate you!" With that she turned and fled from the room as fast as her legs would carry her.

To her surprise, neither Raden nor any of the trolls followed. She ran in circles around the camp, kicking at the dirt and jumping over ditches until her anger turned to weariness. Then she sat in one corner of the unicorn pen and buried her head in her arms.

After a time, something tickled her neck. She swatted at it impatiently. It tickled again. She swatted some more. At the third tickle she gave up and opened her eyes. Wish nickered gleefully and nudged her cheek with a velvety nose.

"Why are you called Wish?" Arica said to the little unicorn as she rubbed behind her ears. "By any chance, do you grant wishes? If so, I'd like to go home."

Wish snorted and nibbled at her pocket.

It was only mid-morning and most of the unicorns, as well as all of the elves, would have been down in the mine. Arica sighed and tried unsuccessfully to push Wish away. The foal's mother stood close by, gazing at Arica with almost human concern. Light was also in the pen, lying on his side. He raised his head toward her.

"I'm sorry, Light," she said. "I wanted to do more, but the power was too strong."

Then once again she knew about the unicorns without being told. Wish's mother was called Song. Light was Wish's father. He had come to this place to rescue more than just her.

You must not be sorry, Light replied. *You did the best you could. That is all one can do.*

"I used to think there was hope," Arica said, gazing out at the dull grey sky and the black-mouthed mountain of stone that rose jaggedly up to reach it. "But now I'm not so sure."

Don't let the prison make you sad, True One, said Song. The unicorn's kindness soothed Arica like a balm.

"Why do you keep calling me that?" Arica wondered, turning toward her. "What do you mean by 'True One'?"

It is what you are, Song replied matter-of-factly.

"What exactly am I?" she asked. "I used to know before I came here. I was an ordinary human girl with a father, mother, grandmother, an aunt and uncle and three cousins. Now I don't know what or where I am, and I'm talking to unicorns, which isn't supposed to happen, and someone is inviting me to rule a world I don't even belong in. I just want to go home!"

You are correct. You have to escape from the evil fairy Raden and take my foal with you, before it's too late.

Arica would have asked her "too late for what?" had not Raden himself arrived the very next moment. He strode arrogantly up to the pen and looked down his nose at Wish. He rattled the silver chains against the post to make sure they would still hold, threw the adult unicorns a look of barefaced contempt, then turned his attention to Arica.

"I take it, then, your answer is no."

"Let me go," said Arica sullenly, glaring up at him. "Let the unicorns go, too. And the elves. You have no right to do this."

"I have every right. You may not have noticed, but I'm in charge here."

"If I say yes, will you let them go?"

"It can be discussed."

Do not trust him, True One, said Song.

"I don't trust you," Arica said to Raden.

His laughter burst into the air. "Smart girl," he said. He nodded to the trolls standing behind him. "Take her," he commanded, "and send her back to the mine."

That night Arica tossed and turned on her bunk, unable to rest, her mind aching with worry. It was easy for her to say that she and Wish should get out of here, but saying it was one thing, doing it quite another.

Sure, there might be ways. First there was the

gate, which was locked and guarded by at least half a dozen trolls at all times. Then there was the fence, which Arica knew was patrolled by trolls. It was also under some kind of magic spell (put there by Raden, no doubt) that worked the same way as a good, old-fashioned jolt of electricity. Arica had seen elves carried away, knocked senseless, after touching it. That left the third way: to sprout wings and fly.

"Stop thrashing around like that, will you?" exclaimed an impatient voice from the dark. "You're keeping me awake!"

"I didn't mean to," Arica said, hoping she sounded suitably sorry.

"Don't be so hard on her," came Drusa's soft voice from the other side. "She's had a hard time of it these past few days."

Perye's face peered at her from above. The welt left by Wish's horn had bruised blue and black, like a tiny ink-splotch against the whiteness of his skin.

"Are you alright, kid?" asked the elf, tousling Arica's hair with his hand.

"I have to get out of here," said Arica, choking down a cry. "I have to go before it's too late."

"We all feel that way," Perye replied, patting her shoulder kindly. "But escaping takes time and the chance of getting away in one piece isn't all that high."

"I have no time," said Arica desperately, trying to

keep her voice from rising hysterically. "The unicorns — " She searched for a way to explain her sense of urgency. "Raden asked me to join with him, and when I refused, he looked like he was going to kill me!"

The pause that followed was long and thick with tension. Arica felt the knots in her stomach tighten painfully as she realized that the elves were still keeping secrets from her — just when she thought she'd finally won their trust. Why wasn't anything around here ever simple and straightforward?

At last Drusa broke the painful silence with a sigh.

"We'd better tell her," she said.

Chapter 8

"Tell me what?" Arica asked.

Perye and Drusa looked at each other the way people do when they know something no one else does.

Through the silence, Arica could hear the snores, moans and restless turning of the elves nearby. Somewhere outside an animal howled as if in pain. A cold wind rattled the windows and door and leaked in through the holes and cracks, chilling her aching muscles. She wished, with a kind of longing that went right through to her bones, that she could be anywhere but here.

"We've been watching you for some time now,"

Perye said. "You're different from other humans, and the unicorns . . . seem to like you."

Arica didn't know how she could ever begin to explain about the unicorns. Since she hardly understood what was going on herself, she settled for avoiding that prickly topic altogether.

"I'm just an ordinary kid," she said. "I go to school and do chores and I don't like to take piano lessons, even though I have to. I'm good at sports, though. Especially soccer. I can run faster than anyone on the team, and I — "

"What is soccer?" asked Drusa.

"That's not what we mean," Perye interrupted. "What we're trying to say is, we believe everything you've said. We can't figure out why Raden is so interested in you, but knowing him, it can't be for any good . . . We're going to let you in on our plans."

"You'll help me, then?" Arica managed to choke out.

Drusa looked at her with pity. "You're a long way from home," she said softly.

Perye continued, "We don't think you're ordinary, by any means. Ordinary humans don't step in front of soothlight or heal dying elves." He frowned, in worry or fear or maybe a little of both. "Whoever you are, and wherever you belong, only the Fairy Queen will know. We have to take you to her before Raden decides you're too much of a threat. Our escape plans weren't meant to be carried out so soon, but it can't be helped. Tomorrow is the night we have chosen."

"I get it. The Fairy Queen will know where the crack is."

"That's right."

"But so does Raden."

"What do you mean?"

"Well, I've seen his living place. The walls are covered with stuffed animals from my home."

Perye rubbed at the furrows in his brow as if they were hurting. "I might as well tell you the worst of it," he said, sighing. "Raden is the Fairy Queen's oldest son. And although she disowned him long ago, he still has a lot of power to go where he wants and get what he wants. He intends to rule in her place. The Fairy Queen's younger son took a dangerous assignment some years ago and never returned. There is no other heir."

"That's not good," Arica said.

"Indeed not," said Perye, turning back to his bed. "But it's not your problem. Your problem is how to get back home. Now let's get some sleep. I'll fill you in on the plans tomorrow."

The following day turned out to be the longest Arica had ever lived through.

It was even worse than the time she'd waited for her father to get back from a business trip so they could go camping in the mountains. She waited in agony for three days but it was worth it in the end. They hiked up a trail to a lake, caught more fish than they could ever possibly eat or carry out, and came face to face with a real mountain lion.

Her brush with the mountain lion seemed like a trip to the petting zoo when she compared it to the events of this past week. She wondered what her father would say if he could see her now.

Arica swung her pickaxe for the thousandth time that morning and coughed dust and dry air from her lungs. Beside her, Wish pranced and bounced like a unicorn on springs. She nudged Arica's bottom with her nose, almost knocking her flat.

True Arica play, she said.

"I can't, Wish," Arica replied, elbowing the foal aside.

Wish was still a child, really. And like a young child, she hindered more than she helped. The little unicorn whinnied, bounced three times, did a circle around the floor, flicked her tail in annoyance, then returned to Arica's side and nudged her again.

"Leave me alone, Wish," she said. "I have to finish what I'm doing."

The last thing Wish intended to do was leave her alone. Throughout that day, she spent more time with Arica than with her own mother. It's just as well, Arica thought to herself. It'll make things a whole lot easier tonight when Song tells her she has to leave with me.

That afternoon, during a brief time by themselves, Perye filled Arica in on all the important details of the plan.

Raden would expect any escape attempt to be made at night, under cover of dark. That was why they would do it just before dusk, while everyone was still eating supper. It made sense: when the elves were all together in the big room, no one would notice if one or two went missing.

While the trolls were busy elsewhere, as was usual that time of day, Perye, Arica and Drusa would slip quietly to the gate. Od would be hidden, waiting, just on the other side.

"Od!" Arica came near to screeching. She stared at Perye like he'd just told her the moons were made of tofu. "He can't be trusted! I know better than anyone! He kidnapped me and he — "

Perye shook his head and put a finger to his lips.

"Calm down and stop howling like a dunked cat or someone will hear. Of course we know he's still working for Raden. That's what he wants everyone to think. But his hatred for Raden is stronger than his loyalty. He and I have been in secret contact for several days now."

As Perye, Arica and Drusa neared the gate, the

plan was, Od would arrive from a different direction and ask the guards to let him leave. Recognizing him, they would undo the bolts. As soon as the gate swung open Od would throw a handful of tearweed in their faces, blinding them for at least five minutes and giving the elves and Arica time to escape through the open gate. There would be horses hidden nearby, provided by Od, of course. They would take the horses and ride away to freedom.

"This plan depends an awful lot upon Od," Arica said uneasily. "I don't care what you say. I don't trust him. He's not the kind of guy to do anything unless there's something in it for him."

"You're right," Perye said, "and there is. Od has been wronged and he wants revenge. He discovered the mine, but Raden is getting all the profits. Od wants us to tell the Fairy Queen what is happening, so that Raden will be stopped."

Somehow this didn't make Arica feel any better, but what could she do? If there was any better way, she couldn't think of it, and besides, anything was better than sitting around doing nothing at all.

It wasn't until they were leaving the mine, the day's work done, that she had the chance to tell Song about the plan.

I'll send my foal to the gate, True One, was all that Song said. But Arica wasn't fooled by the flatness of her expression. She could feel the animal's sorrow inside her like an ache.

Dusk was well on its way when Arica, Perye and Drusa left the building and, keeping to the shadows, slipped quietly toward the gate. Both moons were above the horizon, but they were barely visible through the heavy clouds. A thin, cold wind plucked at their clothes and rustled the leaves of the trees outside the compound.

Wish came silently toward them like a pale ghost, her eyes two black holes against her silver face. For a moment, Arica feared she might bolt away in a flurry of thumping hooves, but the foal came steadily closer. It was plain that Song had told her what and what not to do. Wish trembled under Arica's touch but did not falter or resist being led onward.

No one spoke as they paused only metres from the gate and waited. Arica shivered from fear and cold and wrapped her arms tightly around Wish's slender neck, breathing in the silky-warm scent of unicorn. She sensed that Wish was puzzled but calm; she had total trust in Arica.

Wish doesn't deserve this, Arica thought angrily. She's placing her life in my hands, and she doesn't even know why or what for. I won't let them get her magic. I'll do everything in my power to keep her safe.

The next moment, Od stepped out of the shadows and rapped loudly on the gate.

They waited, hardly breathing. By the sound of things there were at least four guards. If it came to an out-and-out fight that meant one troll for each of them — assuming, of course, that Od was really on their side. She'd believe it when she saw it.

Her stomach lurched at a sudden memory that pushed its way into her mind: Od's battered, accusing stare, after the earthquake at the mine. She leaned toward Perye, a warning on her lips — but it was too late.

The hinges creaked, and Od the troll stepped through the opening. He paused, then turned back toward them.

As Od pulled the handful of tearweed from his pocket, Drusa and Perye darted forward. Arica and the unicorn followed, just as Od threw the tearweed.

At them.

If Arica had taken the time to think, it would have been too late. She drew the magic from Wish's horn before she even realized what she was doing. The next moment a paper-thin, shimmering wall of blue light stood between them and the cloud of tearweed that hurled toward their faces. The tearweed spattered against the wall and fell in a harmless shower to the ground.

"Run!" Arica screamed, as the blue wall popped like a pricked bubble and was gone.

Surprise gave them a head start but not a long

one. In a matter of seconds the trolls' angry shouts could be heard closing in behind them.

Perye and Drusa headed out through the gate in one direction, Arica and Wish in another. The trolls scrambled after them, their swords drawn. They could have been a herd of angry moose for all the thumping going on.

It only took Arica a second to realize that there was no hope of escape, not unless one pair was willing to lead the trolls away from the other. Perye and Drusa had already slipped behind the first rise of ground and had a better, though admittedly poor, chance of getting away.

Arica stopped dead in her tracks and turned around.

"Wish," she said, and the unicorn knew.

The magic spewed from her horn in a streak of blue fire, and sizzled as it struck. Trolls scattered like leaves in an autumn gale. Arica grabbed a sword lost in the scuffle, and nearly dropped it in surprise at its weight. Then she recovered and began swinging. It only took her one good swipe to find that the sword, reaching a certain speed, took off on its own, dragging her right along with it. Metal clanged against metal; she ducked, swung and ducked again. Where was Od?

When she turned to look, it was already too late. She felt the trolls closing in upon her at the same

The trolls scrambled after them, their swords drawn.

moment that she saw Od coming up behind Wish, a silver chain dangling from his upraised hands. The look on the troll's face was one of naked glee at what he was about to do. With a rattle and a clink, the chain encircled the unicorn's head and neck. The blue magic fizzled to extinction; Wish sank weakly to her knees.

This time Arica's stay in the pit was even less pleasant. Raden didn't bother to send along any food and water.

Chapter 9

On Arica's second night in the pit her grandfather paid her a visit.

Though she was thirstier than ever before in her life, and hungry to the point of pain, Arica still had wits enough to remember that her grandfather had been dead since she was four. But imaginary or not, the old fellow took her mind off her suffering and was pleasant to talk to.

Naturally she realized she was only talking to herself, but she'd always heard that talking to yourself wasn't actually harmful as long as you knew it was yourself you were talking to.

Her grandfather just sort of drifted down from

above, settled in a spot in the corner and drew out a small, black pipe. Arica could even smell the sting of smoke as he lit it.

"I've missed you, Arica," her grandfather said.

"I've missed you, too, Grandfather," she managed to croak through cracked lips. "I'm glad you could come."

"Any time," the old man said, puffing with pleasure. "I've seen you looking better, though."

"I've been better," Arica replied.

"Oh, I almost forgot," her grandfather exclaimed, jumping to his feet. Arica watched with interest as her grandfather began digging through each of his pockets. Finally he drew out a leather pouch from one place and a package wrapped in brown paper from another. He handed them both to Arica. The pouch turned out to be full of water. In the paper was a ham and cheese sandwich, neatly sliced in two.

Arica tilted the pouch and began gulping. Gradually she became aware that she was choking and that her grandfather had pulled the pouch away from her over-eager lips.

"Not so fast, my dear," he said with concern. "Just sip it slowly and you'll do better."

So Arica sipped, and took small bites (Grandfather's orders) of the sandwich and listened as her grandfather told wild stories and cackled over his own jokes.

Arica had made up such a lovely and creative image of Grandfather — perfect in every detail, right down to the colour of the old man's socks — that she couldn't help but wonder why she didn't come up with a better-tasting lunch. Say, a cheeseburger, fries with gravy and a chocolate-mint shake. She had never really liked ham, and the cheese tasted sour and stuck in her throat. Oh, well. If this was the best her mind could do, so be it. She had to admit the effect it had was pretty real. She no longer felt thirsty and her hunger was almost gone.

"Arica," said her grandfather, rising to his feet. "I really can't stay. You know how it is — there's so much of this and that to do."

He paused, then looked vaguely around the floor and patted his pockets with his hands like he'd just misplaced something.

"Thanks for the food," Arica said, figuring it never hurt to be polite, even if the person you were thanking wasn't technically real.

"You're welcome," said Grandfather. He gave up on his search and gazed down into Arica's eyes. "I must leave you with a warning, my girl. You'll be rescued soon — within a few hours, I would think. Obey your instincts, for they are good ones, and don't give up. We have high hopes for you."

"Who has high hopes for me, Grandfather?" she asked, but already the old man was gone, snuffed from existence as at the flick of a switch.

"See you later, Grandfather," Arica said, wondering why her mind couldn't have kept up the show for just a little longer. Sighing, she curled up in the least damp, cold corner she could find, worried for the thousandth time about Wish, then closed her eyes in sleep.

Arica awoke to the sound of shouting and the ringing of steel against steel. For one brief, confusing moment she couldn't quite remember where she was or what all the clumping and clashing could mean. Then it came to her — could it be? Could it possibly be the sound of elves in revolt? If it was, then she'd never heard anything so beautiful.

The first thing she did was stand up and start shouting for all she was worth. But her own noise was the smallest of all the noises in the compound. Not only were weapons clanging, but voices howled, feet thumped and rocks rattled against wood that shrieked and splintered.

Then Arica heard the gunshots.

Up to this point she had never heard of guns being used in North Bundelag, not even a hint. But now that she thought about it, Raden did have dealings with the South. Even more importantly, he had hunted in Canada. Raden could be counted on to come up with the best way of killing, no matter where he was — of that Arica was certain. And guns definitely killed better and faster than swords or arrows and bows.

Arica doubled her efforts to make herself heard, but to no avail. She gave up — not because she didn't believe that sooner or later someone would hear her, but because her voice was rapidly fading to a hoarse rasp. Little red lights were beginning to dance in front of her eyes. She groaned, sank down into the grass and leaves, and waited.

The worst part of it was that she wanted to be out fighting — even if it was dangerous and scary — instead of sitting in here uselessly like a lump on a frog's nose. She stood, paced back and forth for a while, then hit the wall with her fist and kicked a spray of leaves into the air. There was a tiny clink as something hit the side of the pit and fell back down.

In a moment Arica had the object in her hand. She stared in surprise at the small black pipe cradled in her palm. Grandfather had been looking for something just before he said goodbye and blinked away. No, it couldn't be. It had all been a dream, the kind you get when you're sick, tired and haven't eaten for days.

But dreams didn't produce realer-than-life pipes that lay in your hand still warm, and ashes that drifted around your feet like silver dust.

True One.

"Yes?" Arica whispered, still staring at the pipe, knowing by now that no matter how quietly she spoke, or from what distance, the unicorns would still hear her. "What is it, Light?"

They are here. We are coming.

Arica laughed aloud with a relief so intense it almost hurt.

"How is Wish? Why hasn't she spoken? Why have none of you spoken until now?" The pipe went into her pocket, forgotten for the moment as a deeper worry flooded her mind. "Is she still alive?"

She lives. We fall silent as our power grows weak.

Terror stabbed at her heart. "You are dying," she said, not even making a question of the words. There had been too much darkness, too much hatred, too much pain.

Not any more, was all the unicorn said.

The minutes dragged like hours. Perhaps it was better not to stand here at the opening like a cook over a bubbling pot. She did three laps around the pit, looked up again and tried to calm herself with a few deep breaths.

The overhead covering lifted. Three noses, three horns and six cocked ears appeared over the rim of the pit. One of the noses dipped down; two brown eyes gleamed at her in joy.

"Wish," she said.

Another head appeared, then another and another.

The heads belonged to unicorns, unicorns she had never seen before. She cried out with joy at seeing them all.

"Who . . . ?" she began, then stopped. There were marks on Wish's neck, left by the silver chains. Had she been bound so tightly that in such a short time — ? No. Why hadn't she thought of it before? Those red welts weren't from pressure. They were burns. Unicorns couldn't bear the touch of silver — it burned right through their hair to the tender flesh beneath.

Raden had punished Wish for defending Arica with magic. But what about all the other unicorns in the camp? Was he punishing them as well? Perhaps, but there was more to it than just that. He had bound them with silver because they were unicorns, wild and free and unafraid of him. The only way he could hold them to himself was with burning silver chains. It was torture — deliberate and malicious.

"No," she said, and felt her insides grow hard and cold as steel. All the pain that Raden had caused would stop now, for she would stop it. She would not allow him to hurt them any more.

By the time Perye and Drusa arrived with a rope to pull her up, Arica knew exactly what she was going to do.

She drew as much power as the unicorns would give her, from each one in turn. They didn't ask what she would use it for, because they already knew — the same way they knew everything she did without being told. The same way she knew everything about them.

She held their magic in the palm of her hand and cradled it like a newly-laid egg — an egg of blazing blue that sent streamers of glittering light through the cracks between her fingers, and made of her hand an incandescent glove.

The mine is empty of the ones called elves, Song informed her. *They have all joined in the fight.*

Arica walked through the centre of the battle, unafraid and untouched. Arrows and spears whizzed past her brow; swords clanged in her ears. Behind her a building toppled. Before her a fire raged. Elves turned and stared as she passed. Trolls ran, screaming out their warnings.

She walked past Raden's dwelling, the smaller building set apart from the others. All gunfire had ceased. But behind those closed and shuttered windows she saw a faint red glow, and felt the stirrings of Raden's awful power as he readied himself for the next round of fighting.

Without even a pause Arica passed on by. Out through a hole in the fence she went, up the long trail to the foot of the ragged mountain with the black hole, where she and the elves and unicorns had slaved and sweated to make this man wealthy.

Arica raised her arm. She'd always been very good at baseball.

The egg of magic arced through the air, like the blazing tip of a comet's tail, and disappeared into the cold, black throat of the mine.

Arica stood and watched — haloed in blue, protected by the unicorns' magic — as the mountain broke in two, then ten, then a thousand exploding pieces that rained to toppling ruins from above. When it was done, there was only the awful silence and the smoke, spilling and spewing into the empty sky.

By the time Arica got back to the compound, most of the trolls had long since fled. Raden was nowhere to be found. There were no slaves or prisoners now, only freed unicorns and elves who wanted to go home.

Wish chooses to stay with you, said Song, dipping her head toward Arica.

"Don't go," Arica pleaded. "Stay with us."

We cannot. We must return to our home in Unicorn Valley, which is several days' journey from here. Our own kind have come to free us and to bring us home. They wait just beyond the nearest hill.

Arica looked at them in amazement. "Did you call them here, and did they hear you all the way from there?"

No, the distance was too great. They came because they felt our need, just as we feel theirs.

"I know what you mean," Arica said softly. She stepped forward and took the mare's nose between her hands, pressing her cheek against the velvety skin.

"I'll take good care of Wish," she whispered past the lump in her throat. "I promise."

Then she turned to face Light.

Thank you, True One, he said, and he, too, lowered his head.

"No, I thank you," she replied.

"For a moment there I'd have sworn she was talking to those unicorns," Perye said to no one in particular. "But I must have been mistaken."

"You must have," said Drusa.

Arica watched until Light and Song were no more than two silver specks against the ridge of hill and sky. Then she turned back to the elves.

"How — ?" she began, but Drusa had already started to explain.

"When you and the baby unicorn were captured," she said, "we changed our plans. We headed for the nearest elf village. They knew all about the mine. When we asked them why they had done nothing to help, they told us the mine was protected by a spell and they hadn't been able to find it for a long time. Finally, they followed a hunting party, but when the spell was lifted to let the trolls in, and they saw the size of the camp, and that Raden himself was always there . . . "

A dark look crossed Perye's face, and he finished for Drusa, "They were afraid."

Drusa shook her head. "They were outnumbered and overpowered. They felt that a botched rescue would be worse than no rescue, because the trolls would be sure to punish the elves inside for the attempt. But when help came — " she paused, and sent a sideways, laughing look to Perye, "and after Perye's inspiring speech, they found all the courage they needed."

"Help?" asked Arica.

Drusa nodded. "The unicorns," she said, her eyes bright with wonder. "They came to help us."

Perye spoke. "We were discussing how we might handle the mine-cloaking spell when a large number of unicorns came into the village at full gallop. They circled for a while. They seemed . . . well, anyway, I hailed one of them."

He grinned at Arica, looking very pleased with himself, and continued, "I didn't know how to make them understand me. I asked, 'Are you looking for the place where some of your kind are being held in captivity?' They stopped circling and just stood there, watching me. I felt I should try another way, so I closed my eyes and pictured the mine in my head, particularly the unicorn pen."

Perye paused, then shivered. "When I opened my eyes, the unicorns were circling again, and tossing their heads. They looked angry, and impatient to go. I called for everyone to get their weapons, and we all — elves and unicorns together — headed back to the mine in a band."

Drusa's voice was filled with excitement. "The unicorns held themselves to our pace, even though it was clear they wanted to go faster. Perye and I led everyone to where we thought the mine was, and the unicorns' magic pierced the illusion. They also used their magic against the trolls at the gate, helping us to overpower them."

"We freed everyone we could," said Perye. "When the prisoners saw what we were up to, they joined in the fight."

"Thank you," Arica said, "for coming back."

"What else could we do?" said Drusa, and hugged her.

Perye cleared his throat. "Should we go?" he asked. His teeth flashed white in a face blackened by dust and grime.

"Gladly," said Arica. "Where to?"

"To the Fairy Queen," replied Drusa. "To send you home."

Chapter 10

"I think you have some explaining to do," Perye said as they walked.

They were wading through waist-high grass under a watery sun that threw out plenty of pale shadows, but no warmth. Wildflowers covered the hilltops in garlands of red and mauve. Birds of all kinds peppered the sky overhead. Their cries shrilled in the air, discordant notes that sweetened as they fell. Flies whizzed past Arica's face; mosquitoes circled near her ears. She took an angry swat at one of them and missed.

"It figures," she complained to the elves. "I come all this way to a totally new place that no one has ever heard of before, and what do I find? Common houseflies! Ordinary mosquitoes!" She sighed. "I guess some things are just meant to be, no matter where you go."

"You're not answering me," said Perye sharply, throwing her a glare.

"I don't know what you mean," Arica replied, knowing full well what he meant. "How much farther do we have to go?"

"I'm talking about you blowing up the mine with magic," Perye said, as through a mouthful of grit. "How did you do it? You might not have thought of this, but you're not supposed to be able to do things like that. I've never even heard of a fairy pulling off such a stunt, let alone a skinny, half-grown human female. And I've done a lot of studying about magic over the years. I'm waiting for you to explain. What do you have to say for yourself?"

Arica didn't dare meet the elf's searing green gaze. Instead she focused on the antics of Wish, as the foal chased a frightened blue butterfly through a patch of prairie blossoms.

"I don't know how I did it," Arica mumbled into her chest, wondering if now would be a good time to take off through the tulips with Wish. "I was angry. It just came to me, that's all."

"Well, remind me not to get in the way the next time something 'just comes to you.' "

Arica glanced up just in time to catch the end of one of Drusa's smiles. Her eyes, unlike Perye's fierce, brooding stare, glowed with the joy of being alive as she mouthed a "thank you." Arica smiled back, her heart lifting, and decided that if Drusa wasn't going to take Perye's grumbling seriously, then neither would she.

She turned back to Perye. "Do you wish I hadn't done it, then?"

"I didn't say that."

"Let's just forget it," interrupted Drusa, stepping between them. "We have escaped. We're free. Nothing else matters. You make everything harder than it is, Perye. You analyze things to death. What Arica did or didn't do, and what she is or isn't, is for the Fairy Queen to decide."

By evening they had arrived at the river. To Arica's delight she could still hear the music. But it seemed different, somehow. Less soothing, and with a certain note of urgency.

Deciding she must be fooling herself — anyone would feel uneasy after what she'd been through — she knelt at the water's edge to wash the dust and grime from her skin and clothes. Wish slurped and splashed beside her; the elves dabbled and dipped. Overhead, a flock of silver swallows fluttered under the rising moons. Arica scooped up handfuls of

Wish slurped and splashed beside her . . .

water and flung them at Wish. The next moment she was pinned beneath two hooves, nearly covered in water, howling for mercy. She couldn't remember when she'd ever been so happy.

For supper they ate wild blueberries and a plant Drusa called a root willow. It reminded Arica of baked potatoes, only sweeter and not so dry. They slept with their backs to a bluff, hiding themselves as well as they could, and took turns keeping watch.

By noon of the next day they had arrived at the forest's edge.

"We'll enter here heading in a southeast direction," Perye explained. "If all goes well we should cross the main path in less than an hour. We'll follow it all the way through, and hopefully we'll be out by late afternoon. Any questions?"

"Yes," said Arica. "Are there any wolves in these woods?" She wasn't sure why this unpleasant idea had suddenly come unbidden to her mind. Perhaps it was because in every fairy story she'd every read involving forests, there always seemed to be wolves inside them, waiting to pounce on unsuspecting children.

"Wolves?" Perye asked, looking surprised that she'd even asked. "Of course there are wolves. There are always wolves. But they're the least of our problems.

for."

"Wolves? And bears?" Arica practically wailed. She wondered why no one had bothered to mention, in the dozen or so days since she'd been here, that there might possibly be such things as wolves and bears in Bundelag. It made her wonder what other information had been left out of conversations, passed over, not brought up.

As for this business about wolves being the least of their problems — well, let him just once come face-to-face with a snarling pack. See if that didn't change his opinion.

Then suddenly the whole situation struck her as funny. Here she was, standing in a forest with a unicorn and two elves, in search of one fairy, fleeing from another, being chased by trolls and calmly talking about wolves, bears and snakes with wings. If her parents could see her now . . .

An hour later Perye told them they were lost.

The first sign that something had gone wrong was the fact that they hadn't found the main trail leading through the forest.

"We should have run into it by now," Perye said, leaning against an old, half-rotted tree and scratching his chin. "I could have sworn it was right here somewhere."

They stood together in puzzled silence. Overhead a bird cawed. Leaves rustled; a twig snapped deep inside the undergrowth. Arica peered into the shadows, seeing nothing. Everything was blending into a tiresome sameness, and she couldn't have told one clump of trees from the next if her life depended on it.

Wish snorted, leaped over a twig, pirouetted through a patch of yellow daisies and ended up at her side. Her startled eyes stared into Arica's. Under her touch, the unicorn's muscles trembled.

"What is it, Wish?" she asked, rubbing the unicorn's back.

True Arica go.

"If only we could speak to unicorns," Drusa said, looking at Wish in a wistful kind of way. "They're so much wiser and aware of danger than we are."

Perye threw Arica a scorching glare that clearly dared her to admit to something. Arica cleared her throat and suddenly became very interested in a little red bug making its way slowly across a leaf. He had guessed about the talking in her head, that was for sure. But how could she explain it to him when she didn't understand it herself? She sure hoped the Fairy Queen — when they finally found her — could give her some answers.

"Let's get out of here," Perye said finally, looking around uneasily. "We just haven't gone far enough, that's all."

Half an hour later he admitted they'd gone far enough, but they kept on for lack of anything better to do.

A half hour after that they arrived back at the same patch of yellow flowers and the same scarecrow tree Perye had leaned against before. Drusa took one look at it all, sank down onto a stump and put her face in her hands.

"All right," Perye said, half to himself. "Now what should we do?"

Drusa wiped her eyes with her sleeve, produced one final sniff and raised her chin bravely.

Bad magic, said Wish in Arica's mind.

"Let's think this through logically," Perye mused. "It's clear that we're going around in circles, but how is it happening?"

Magic bad, said Wish.

"We're under a spell," Arica said, suddenly figuring out what Wish was trying to say. "Think about it for a minute. We know where we're going but we can't get there. Raden has cast a spell over us and we're stuck in the forest."

"Of course," said Drusa, wide-eyed and fearful. "He wouldn't let us go without a fight, would he? Not after what we did."

"That's a good theory," admitted Perye. "It might just be true."

Arica and Drusa sat in woeful silence while Wish danced through the flowers, sniffing at the leaves, and Perye paced back and forth, deep in thought.

What little Arica knew about spells and spell casting had come from the stories her grandmother had told her. There were rules about spells that appeared in all the fairy tales. And one of the rules was that every spell could be broken. In every story she could recall, there was always a loophole or a means of escape. It was just a matter of finding it, that was all.

In the end it was Wish who came up with the answer.

Arica never did find out if it was an accident, or if the little unicorn knew all along. Whatever the case, Wish suddenly started nipping at everything in sight — first the leaves, then the flowers, the butterflies, the birds and finally at Arica herself. She nuzzled her face, nibbled her shirt, then plucked at her pockets with her teeth. One jacket pocket, pulled completely inside out by her efforts, emptied its contents onto the ground at Arica's feet. She saw a ring, a pencil, two quarters and a dime from home, and her dead grandfather's pipe.

She picked up the pipe and held it flat in her palm. She had forgotten all about it. Then, right before her eyes, the pipe turned in her hand like the needle of a compass pointing toward some distant pole.

She turned it back.

It moved again, ending up in exactly the same place as before.

"Where did you get the pipe?" Drusa asked, moving in for a closer look. "It must hold some kind of counterspell."

"If that's true," Perye stated, peering over her shoulder, "then it should lead us out of here."

"What's a counterspell?" asked Arica.

"It's a spell cast by someone to cancel out another spell . . . " Drusa started to explain.

The crash and roar that followed took all thoughts of spells from their minds and sent them scrambling. They ran until long after the forest grew silent behind them.

"The bears are grouping," was all Perye had to say. "It makes them all the more dangerous."

Arica shivered. "Are you sure it wasn't wolves?" she asked.

"I'm sure," he replied. "Wolves are always silent when they hunt. With wolves, you'd never know what hit you."

"Thanks for telling me that," Arica muttered under her breath. "It makes me feel so much better."

What seemed like hours later, Perye agreed to let them slow to a walk. Several times the pipe turned in Arica's hand, forcing them to correct their course as the spell pulled them off track.

By nightfall they had passed out of the forest. There they huddled, leaning upon one another, hungry and bone-tired. They stared in fright at the dark and dour sight that stretched out before them, from one black horizon to the next.

"It's called the Badlands," said Perye, his words thick with fatigue. "The Fairy Queen lives on the other side."

Chapter 11

Arica had never seen anything so frightening, not even in her wildest nightmare.

The landscape appeared to have been dipped in soot. Sickly trees dotted the countryside like twisted, crippled limbs. Weeds grew here and there in tattered clumps. Beyond all of this the evening sky hung low, only a little less black and dismal than everything beneath it. Arica stared, not daring to believe what her eyes were telling her.

"I'm ready to wake up now," she said to no one in particular. "Any time would be fine."

"I hate to say it, but this is all as real as you are," Perye informed her.

"They say magic doesn't work in the Badlands," Drusa said. "It's too bad — " She paused, as though the next words were somehow stuck in her throat.

"Let me guess," said Arica. "What you were going to say was, it's too bad no one's lived to confirm it."

"No one I know of," Drusa admitted.

The fact did nothing to lift Arica's spirits as they got ready for sleep. The feeling that came from those eerie, empty hills kept her tossing late into the night. She stared up at the two pale moons and listened to Wish wheeze peacefully on one side of her and Perye snore noisily on the other. Later she took her turn at the watch, relieving Drusa, but it wasn't until well into Perye's shift that her weariness finally got the best of her, and she slept.

Naturally, she dreamed of her grandfather.

The old man was even more gleeful and lively than ever. This annoyed Arica, who was tired, cross and frightened out of her wits of the Badlands, which had managed to work their way into her dream with terrible clarity. In sleep, her imagination went to work, sharpening and deepening the hills, filling them with more unspeakable creatures and horrific perils than they could possibly hold. Her grandfather grinned at her as if the whole thing were wildly amusing, paced back and forth a few times, shared a joke with Wish, then settled upon a flat-topped rock and held out his hand.

"My pipe, please," he said politely.

Arica held on to it stubbornly. Dream or no dream, she might as well use it to get some answers.

"Not until you explain some things," she said firmly, sitting up and crossing her arms. She raised her chin to the air with what she felt was just the right amount of indignation.

Her grandfather didn't even have the grace to look surprised. He crossed his arms right back, and his legs as well.

"I was wondering when you'd start getting wise to me," he said matter-of-factly.

"Are you dead or alive?" she demanded.

"That's an interesting question," replied Grandfather. "One that I've often thought about."

"You're not answering my — "

Arica stopped. Grandfather was starting to disappear. She could see right through his body to the bushes beyond.

"Give me the pipe, please," Grandfather said pleasantly. "You don't need it any more and I must go. I have business elsewhere."

"It's not polite to fade when someone is still talking!" Arica snapped back.

His laughter was like she remembered, like the rumble of falling rock, like bursting bubbles, like the patter of rain on a roof.

The next moment Wish plucked the pipe from Arica's hand, pranced in a little circle around the rock, flicked her tail at the dark trees, then dropped the pipe into Grandfather's outstretched hand.

"Thank you, Wish," the old man said, rubbing the unicorn's nose. "Take good care of my girl, will you?" With that he blinked out of existence.

Arica awoke lying next to Wish, her arms wound in a fierce lock about the animal's neck.

Angry don't be, True Arica, the little unicorn said inside her head.

"I'm not, Wish," she said. "It's just that he can be so annoying. Especially for someone who isn't real."

Arica checked the pocket of her jacket. The pipe, of course, was gone.

Arica forgot all about her dream when they entered the Badlands.

The first thing she noticed was the heat. Going by what she'd learned in science class at school, it was due to the thin layer of black soot that lay over everything — ground, rocks, hills and what little plant life had managed to gasp its way up through the sludge. Heat soaked into the colour black, she had been taught, but bounced right off anything that was white. She gazed around. There was nothing any lighter than dark grey as far as the eye could see.

To make matters worse, the soot rose in great

billows around them with every step they took. It settled into ears, eyes, nose and hair, mixing with sweat and working its way under clothing, and into cracks and pores. After the first hour Arica became certain nothing could ever be as bad as this.

That's when they came to the river. It was the only truly black river Arica had ever seen, and it didn't sing. It screamed.

The screams weren't ones you could actually hear, of course, and neither were the words. They existed somewhere beyond the range of ordinary sound, deep inside her mind. She couldn't have told anyone exactly what the river said, only that the meaning was bitter and full of self-pity. And the river wanted something, something that no one was willing to give.

The silent howls raged on and on in her brain as she stared down upon the river. It twisted through ragged channels like a dark, destructive snake, shrieking as it went. Arica sagged weakly against Wish, shivering in horror and fear.

"Can you feel it, Wish?" she whispered, winding her arms tightly about the unicorn's neck.

Bad water, said Wish.

"Yes, very bad," Arica agreed, shivering.

"Thankfully we don't have to cross it," Perye said, answering their unvoiced question. "However, it's said that the easiest way through this area is to follow the river."

Then as they paused and the dust settled around them, Arica looked back across the sinister wasteland they had just passed through and saw another, much larger cloud off in the distance.

"It's Raden and his trolls," she said to thè elves beside her.

"Yes," Perye agreed, squinting out from under his hand. "They're catching up."

Panic caught in her throat. Never again would she complain to her parents about having to come in at night or going to bed on time. She wished they would call her now, into warmth and safety, out of this land they had never heard of, away from the hundred trolls on her tail and the river that wanted to swallow her whole.

"Let's get out of here," said Drusa, moving forward. "The longer we stand around, the closer they get."

They made good progress, until Wish pulled up lame. It only took Arica a few minutes to pry the sharp rock out of her hoof, but in that short time Raden and his trolls gained a startling amount of ground.

Then it seemed the more she and the elves hurried, the slower they went. It made Arica think of one of those slow-motion dreams where the faster you run the farther behind you get, until you're hardly moving at all. Only this was much more frightening than a dream could ever be.

"Run!" Perye screamed, when there was nothing else to do.

They ran — until their throats grew dry and raw and their legs burned and their hearts pounded in their chests. In the end they found themselves standing at the edge of a cliff — the river shrieking and twisting through the canyon below them — surrounded by trolls, staring up the barrel of Raden's cold, black gun.

"At last," the fairy growled, pointing the weapon directly at Arica. "Now you are mine."

Her stomach flipped into her throat. She tried to move, to speak, to do anything at all, but her body refused to obey. She remembered her father saying that when you're scared, the best thing to do is pause and take a few deep breaths. At the time he'd been referring to playing piano in public, but she'd give it a try.

Just as she'd thought — it actually made things worse. Dizziness swept through her; the ground tilted wildly. Wish stood to one side of her, her four hooves firmly planted, while Arica clung weakly to her neck. Drusa held her on the other side.

"Wait," Perye said to Raden, holding up one hand. "Let's talk this over."

"He doesn't want to kill you," said Drusa quietly. "Not really. He just wants you under his control."

"There's nothing to talk about," Raden snapped,

ignoring Drusa. His finger tightened on the trigger.

Arica thought fast. Raden didn't want the elves or the unicorn. The one he was really after was her. With any luck, with her out of the way he'd let the others go.

Would he kill her? Arica wasn't sure. He wanted her for something, that was certain. Perhaps he wanted her because of the unicorns. If that was the case, she'd rather die.

Wish knew right away what she was up to and followed without question. Arica turned, leaped and fell, all in one fluid motion.

Behind her Perye shouted: "No!"

She heard Drusa scream her name.

Then she and Wish entered the water. It was like plunging into a pool of quicksand.

Arica held her breath as she tried to swim upward to the surface. Her arms seemed pinned to her sides; her legs felt tied in place, unable to bend or kick. She pushed with every ounce of her strength, once, twice, three times, and drifted up a mere centimetre, maybe two.

The river wouldn't let her go. She could feel the sludgy liquid around her like something alive — gripping, clutching, squeezing the life from her body.

"Oh no, Wish," she silently cried. "What have I done?"

Then the world fell out from under her.

Chapter 12

At least Arica could almost breathe again. Angry water roared all around her as she tumbled downward with the waterfall, legs sprawled and kicking, hands clutching at jagged rocks. A mucky black pool churned below her. The branch of a tree whipped by her face, then another. Then one caught her middle with a snapping sound. What little breath she had left was driven from her lungs in a painful whoosh. She dangled a few metres above the pool, clutching desperately to the tree that had saved her.

She hardly dared to blink as the scraggy, leafless tree groaned and swayed beneath her weight. At last it steadied enough to allow her a quick look around.

No big deal. All she had to do was grab hold of that larger tree above her head, swing over to that sharp-looking rock, then crawl up that big branch attached to a tree on the bank. All, of course, with the mud pounding down on her, coating her and everything else in slimy mush.

The river howled beneath her, splashing and pulling at her feet. She moved slowly, with great care. Up, up and over she reached. Grabbing the next tree was like putting soapy hands on a door-knob. She got it, and swung, her feet landing on the rock. She teetered, the tree slid from her grasp and she crouched there, trembling.

The final phase of her efforts turned out to be the hardest part, for the branch grew outward and down from the stunted trunk on the riverbank. She was forced to climb uphill. For every ten centimetres she moved forward, she slid back eight or nine — all the while skidding wildly to one side or the other. But finally she was there. She gripped handfuls of half-dead weeds, pulled herself over the lip of the bank and flopped face down into the soot and slime.

Arica lay without moving, wracked with coughs. She stretched her cramped and aching muscles, moaned in agony, then rolled over, opened her eyes and stared up into the cold, black gaze of Raden.

She covered her eyes and waited for the sound of a gun being cocked.

The river howled beneath her, splashing and pulling at her feet.

It never came.

"That was certainly entertaining," came the harsh, grating voice above her head. "And it gave me time to think. Shooting you would be too easy. I've decided to take you and your pathetic little elf friends back to the mine. I have plans for you."

"You're so kind," Arica said from the weed patch.

"Bring her!" he barked at the trolls, and turned away.

Rough hands hauled her to her feet. Sure enough, there were Drusa and Perye, their hands bound behind their backs. Her eyes travelled over the group of trolls. Thank goodness there was no small white unicorn to be seen. Not that this was a good sign — Wish could just as easily be lying in the pool of slime at the bottom of the black river. But she wasn't going to let herself think like that, not even for a second.

By mid-afternoon they had left the Badlands behind.

Without even a pause for rest, Raden led the group on into the forest. Inside, the darkness closed over them like a lid. After the Badlands, being in the forest should have been a relief. While travelling with Perye, Drusa and Wish, Arica had enjoyed the great variety of wildlife and the many sounds that went along with them. But now these were drowned out by the noise of the trolls stomping, thumping and complaining at every turn, and by Raden barking out orders and banging things together — actions that seemed to give him great pleasure.

It was beyond her why the trolls stayed with him in the first place. It was plain as the warts on their lumpy noses that they didn't like him, and he certainly acted like he couldn't stand the sight of them. What was keeping them with him? she wondered. He was using them, obviously, and paying them — maybe even paying them well. But was it worth being treated like the hind end of a mule just for money? Surely there were easier and more pleasant ways of earning a living than this.

It wasn't until they stopped in a clearing for a rest and something to eat, at what Arica's stomach told her must surely be suppertime, that the group finally fell silent. The trolls feasted on bread, dried fruit and meat from their pouches, then drank from the waterskins. But no one offered any to her or the elves. Her mouth was so dry she could have spit up a pocketful of cotton-tree fluff, and her stomach moaned unhappily beneath her ribs. She was just about to stop pretending she wasn't half-starved and ask the nearest troll for a bite, when a voice like piping flutes sounded in her head.

True Arica, Wish said. *I come, rescue. So close.*

After the first surge of joy at knowing the unicorn was still alive, a flood of raw fear nearly overcame her.

Not now, Wish, she thought in panic, staring wildly around. There are too many of them!

Too many, not, Wish replied firmly. *Help with me.*

It only took Arica a moment to realize that Wish had heard her unspoken thoughts as if she had shouted them right out loud. Her heart knocked inside her chest. She sucked in a breath to steady herself, then looked up to see several of the trolls staring suspiciously in her direction.

Get a grip, Arica, she said to herself.

What is grip? asked Wish, like bells inside her head. *Get where?*

Never mind, Wish, she thought back, still not believing this was really happening. Did you say you have help? Do you have a plan?

No plan. Help. Come.

Arica bit her tongue to keep from howling out loud. She reminded herself that Wish was only a child, hardly more than a baby. It was true she was a magical creature, extremely intelligent and practically immortal, who when grown would command the respect of every other being in the land. But at the moment Arica felt more like swatting her on the rump than anything else.

What is your plan, Wish? she repeated, wondering if thoughts could sound as though squeezed through gritted teeth.

We come.

Nothing to do but wait, then. It was clear she'd get nothing sensible from Wish.

The trolls' meal was over. Some of them lay stretched on patches of forest moss, dozing. Others were gathering up the waterskins and what crumbs of food were left upon the ground. Still nobody had offered a thing to her or the elves.

Perye and Drusa sat on the opposite side of the clearing, their faces smudged with soot, their clothing soiled and torn, their green eyes bright with anger. She figured she didn't look much better, with the added effect of caked-on river mud and soggy clothing. She thought of slipping over quietly to tell them about the rescue plan, then wondered exactly how that would help. Likely it would only draw unwanted attention to her and to them. Better to let the elves act when the moment came.

She sat, outwardly calm but inwardly boiling, and studied the tiresome progress of a line of ants across a piece of bark. Sunlight flickered through the leaves above her head, making patterns of dark and light against her skin. Birds fluttered, then lighted silently among the boughs.

Arica shuddered, though not with cold. Something about this forest felt wrong to her, and to put it in plain English — or whatever language she was speaking in this place — it made her want to scream and run. She should be hearing birds chirping and squirrels chattering, even (and she could hardly believe she was missing this) a mosquito or two whining in her ears. But not this thick, heavy, smothering silence that filled her soul with dread.

Raden moved toward her. She turned the other way as he towered over her, looking down.

"What is it, little girl?" he said in his harsh, taunting way. "Something making you nervous?"

"I don't like how the forest feels," she mumbled, still not meeting his glowering stare.

So that's how it happened that Raden was standing right next to her when Wish bounded eagerly out from among the trees and into the clearing.

Raden saw the unicorn and stiffened. The trolls snapped to attention, many drawing swords. Perye and Drusa jumped to their feet, their eyes brightening with hope and surprise.

And out from the deepest, darkest part of that deathly-still forest a shadow moved, joined by another and another and yet another. Like dark pieces torn from the forest's black heart they came, drifting, spreading, without sound or substance, until at last they ringed the clearing like a ghostly squad.

Wish had managed to find some wolves.

Chapter 13

Arica jumped but Raden moved faster. In a flash he had her left arm twisted up behind her back and one of his own in a lock about her throat.

The wolves stood in silence, not moving. A dozen pairs of yellow eyes gleamed in the shadows. A dozen mouths gaped, tongues dangling wetly between iron jaws. Teeth glistened, spiked and yellow, set in snarling red. All eyes were fixed, unblinking, on Arica and Raden, as they waited for what would happen next.

They didn't have long to wait.

"I've got the girl," Raden shouted at the unicorn. "Call off the wolves, or else!"

Arica didn't want to think what the "or else" might mean but she knew something had to be done soon. Raden's grip on her neck was getting tighter and tighter, making breathing nearly impossible. On the bright side, he couldn't very well kill her yet, or he'd have nothing left to bargain with.

Wish reared up on her hind legs and pawed the air, flinging her head from side to side. A low rumble came from the throats of the wolves. The trolls nearest to them shuffled backward, moaning with fright. Raden remained where he stood with Arica clutched tightly in his arms.

"We'll never get anywhere like this," he called to the unicorn. Amazingly, he sounded almost pleasant, almost reasonable. A shiver went down her spine, like cold fingers. She liked him better the other way.

Want what? said Wish in Arica's mind.

"Wish . . . wonders what . . . you want," Arica managed to wheeze out past the choke hold.

The fairy's body stiffened behind her. "That thing talks to you?" he barked in surprise.

For a moment Arica almost thought she heard fear in his voice. But no, she must have been mistaken, for he continued on, as coldly polite as ever.

"It's plain to see we have a no-win situation here," Raden said in his eerie, logical way. "I'm suggesting," and he paused, meeting Wish's gentle gaze, "that you call off the wolves. You go as well. I'll send the trolls away and set the elves free. After all, this is really between me and the girl. Leave us alone to work out our differences."

"You mean, leave you alone to slit her throat!" Perye shouted as he lunged. Then, because of his bonds and a rather large twig, he tripped and fell flat on his face.

"I promise not to threaten her life again, if that makes you feel better," Raden continued. "Send the wolves after the trolls to make sure they do as I tell them. You can trust me to keep my word."

"Trust!" guffawed Drusa, practically choking.

Agree, said Wish.

"Don't leave me, Wish!" Arica wailed in panic. What had gone wrong here? Had Wish lost her mind? Had Raden cast a spell over her?

No choice.

"You can't do this! He's a maniac! He won't do anything he says!"

No choice.

Wish turned and faded quietly into the trees, like a dream suddenly vanished and already half-forgotten. The wolves, too, were no longer in sight.

"You'll never get away with this!" Arica screamed at Raden. "Wish will be close by, hiding in the forest! She'll never let you kill me!"

His laugh was staccato hard, like nails bouncing

off an old tin roof. "For a girl who's in so thick with unicorns, I'm amazed you didn't know. Too bad, but you're wrong. A unicorn never lies."

She saw through a numb haze that the trolls had cut Perye and Drusa free and were shoving them toward the trees. Raden let Arica go so suddenly she fell to her knees. Drusa broke away and came running toward her. She lifted Arica up, held her and pressed the girl's head to her shoulder.

"Is it true?" Arica cried, tears squeezing out from between her tightened lids.

"Yes," whispered Drusa sadly, "it's true. A unicorn must always keep a promise. It's part of the magic, part of what they are. They are Truth."

Then Perye, who had gone back into the trees, reappeared and took her in his arms. The hug was over almost before it began, but as he pulled away she felt him slip something thin and sharp into the pocket of her jacket.

After that the elves, too, were gone, and she stood alone in the forest with Raden and nothing but the silence and her own fear pounding in her throat.

Within the hour they arrived at the forest's edge. Raden had been watching too carefully for her to remove the object from her pocket, but by the shape she judged it to be a knife or dagger of some sort. Something, at least, to protect herself against the attack when it came. But she couldn't help thinking she'd be no better off than a mouse squeaking at the feet of a charging lion.

The evening was clear and warm and it seemed, as she gazed out across the landscape, that she had never seen anything quite so grand. In the west, sunlight slanted through the gauzy clouds like banners of pink and gold. Overhead, the birds of Bundelag sang praises to the glory of the dying day.

A plan was beginning to form somewhere in the back of her mind. She had almost escaped from Raden once by jumping into water, so why not again? When they reached the musical river and stopped for a drink, which they would sooner or later, it would be dark. Dark enough, hopefully, for her to sit close to the riverbank. Then, when Raden took his eyes off her, which he certainly had to at some point, she would plunge over the bank and into the water. She could swim well, and a river that sparkled cleanly over the rocks would surely carry her away to freedom.

Arica smiled to herself. Her heart lifted. She was less annoyed than usual when Raden stopped suddenly, scowled at something off in the distance, then reached out with one hand and grabbed her roughly by the arm.

"Ouch!" she said, swatting at him with the palm of her hand.

"Be quiet, you little fool!" he snapped, glaring

down at her like she'd just crawled up from some slimy hole.

Arica stopped walking, mainly because she had no choice, and followed the direction of his gaze. There was indeed something out there, but it was awfully far away.

"A deer," she said.

"No," he growled. "Too large."

"An elk?"

"There are no elk in Bundelag," he sneered. "And who gave you permission to offer an opinion?"

"I don't need — " she began, and then she knew. Somehow she was part of them, as they were part of her — the way it had been, it seemed, since the start of time. She would always know when a unicorn was near.

Raden saw it in her eyes. He stared, the rage burning darkly in his face, then stepped back and drew the soothstone from his pocket. It glowed in his palm — ugly and red and swollen, like something too unnatural to be real. The wind screamed in terror, then stilled. The birds fell silent. Arica's heart knocked painfully beneath her ribs.

She backed away from Raden, looking wildly around for a means of escape. There were no trees to hide behind, no caves to crawl into. Not a rock or a shrub in sight. The fairy's eyes were locked upon her as she stumbled backward in an attempt to get away.

His hand was held high, the stone pointed at her chest. It pulsed with light as if in time to the beat of her own heart. Was it her imagination? Was her fear making her lose her mind? She could have sworn the stone whispered her name.

Then her hand fell to her side, and she remembered Perye's knife.

Arica crouched and drew the weapon from her pocket in one swift motion. Raden's face grew deathly white and he paused, the air hissing through his teeth. She glanced at the object in her hand to gauge its size and shape, to determine the best way to use it. She almost dropped it, her arms weak with surprise, when she saw what it was.

It was not a knife, after all. It wasn't a dagger, either, nor even a small sword.

It was Wish's tiny golden horn.

Even as she stared at it — her mind screaming against the thought that Wish had died with the giving — the horn began to glow pale and blue beneath her fingers. Then the magic came. It tingled up her arm, filled her chest with warmth, slowed and steadied her heart, then ran through her whole body from tip to toe. She raised her eyes to her enemy, strong and unafraid.

"Thank you, Wish," she said, and struck.

Bolts of raw power crackled in the air and slapped into the ground around her feet. Birds rose, cawing in terror. Small creatures scattered and dived into holes. Grass and dirt sprayed upward, scooped and tossed about by pure electric magic. The air swirled, a kaleidoscope of red and blue, twisting around her head, while the power spit and howled in her ears and shivered across her skin.

It wasn't long before Arica knew she could not possibly win. Raden was a fairy fully-grown, native to this world and wise in the use of magic. His power was drawn from the bottomless depths of the earth on which they stood. Her power came from the tiny gold horn of one very small unicorn who had given her all, with love and hope. It should have been enough, but it wasn't. Arica knew very well that life didn't work that way. Just because you were good or right or true didn't mean you would always win. She had learned that lesson long ago in another world.

As the blue light in the horn grew weaker and weaker, and with it her strength and hope, a small idea formed somewhere in the back of her mind. She considered it. Instead of trying to overpower the evil, perhaps she could simply absorb it — suck the rock dry, so to speak.

She raised Wish's battered horn one final time, and instead of striking the stone, she merely touched it gently with the horn's tip.

And told the horn to pull the magic into itself.

There was a flash of red light that nearly blinded

her. Raden jumped backward, shrieking, but already it was too late. The horn pulsed crimson, sucking power, then shattered with a crash that rattled the very bones of the earth and tumbled them both end-over-end across the ground.

When Arica opened her eyes, the horn was gone. The stone lay where it had fallen, dull and faintly throbbing.

Raden rose to his knees, howled in rage and lunged, his hands outstretched and reaching.

Chapter 14

The hands never arrived.

Raden stopped almost on top of her, still on his knees with his arms held out. He was frozen in place, like a statue carved of cloth and flesh. His rage-filled eyes stared sightlessly into hers.

Arica slid out from under his body and rolled. When she'd gone far enough to feel safe, she scrambled to her feet. Raden still hadn't moved. She turned to flee — and came face to face with elves.

Perye and Drusa were riding a dapple-grey stallion. The thrill of seeing them faded into a blaze of wilder emotion, as she stared at the unicorn and at the woman who sat majestically upon him.

It was Light, mate of Song and father of her own dear Wish. The lady upon his back was someone she'd thought she'd never see again. She wore a purple cloak and had a painted stick held outward like a wand, still pointing at the man on his knees. The look on her face could have set a house on fire.

"Grandmother!" Arica cried, and flung herself at the woman's feet.

Then somehow Grandmother had dismounted and was taking Arica in her arms, and Arica was crying and holding her like she'd never let her go. After a while Grandmother gently pushed her away, put a finger under her chin and gazed fondly at her wet, upturned face.

"My dear, you've had quite an adventure," she said with affection.

"You came, Grandmother!" Arica cried.

Grandmother raised her head. Light met her look and tossed his head.

"I was brought," she said quietly. "This is the first time I have been honoured in this way. Thank you, my friend."

Then Grandmother announced in a queenly-sounding voice, "The foal can return. The pact is broken."

There was a flash of light and Wish appeared out of nowhere. She bounded up to Arica and began nibbling at her fingers, nuzzling her ear, and pushing

She wore a purple cloak and had a painted stick held outward like a wand . . .

and shoving until Arica finally gave in. She threw her arms around the unicorn's neck and planted a series of loud, joyous kisses upon her face and nose.

"Oh, Wish," she said, laughing in sheer happiness. "You're the best!"

True Arica, said Wish. *Love.*

Then Arica remembered. She pulled back and stared at that place in the centre of Wish's forehead. A few drops of dry blood still clung to the unicorn's brow.

I broke. Hurt, Wish explained.

"I'm so sorry," Arica managed to whisper through a throat thick with sadness.

It's alright, True One, Light assured her. *Her pain is over now, and she has only lost the magic for a time. She's still a baby. A new horn will grow. Touch her face and you'll see. One begins already.*

Arica's fingers moved up under the lock of silver mane that fell across Wish's forehead. Sure enough, a small, hard lump had already begun to form. It tingled under her touch.

"Thank you for saving my life, Wish," she whispered into the unicorn's ear.

Perye and Drusa slid from the back of the grey and came toward her.

"Thank you both," Arica said, "for everything."

Perye cleared his throat, as if to say something, then stopped. Drusa took Arica's hand in hers, her eyes wide and serious.

"Do you know who your grandmother is?" she asked in a quiet voice.

"Of course. She's . . . " Arica turned and looked at her grandmother. Her grandmother gazed back at her, and at Wish, with an expression so intense that Arica was caught in it, unable to look away.

"I am the Fairy Queen of North Bundelag," Grandmother said. "Your father is my younger son. He chose to marry a human and to live in her world. He has forgotten everything he knew about this place. This has caused me much sorrow, even though he is happy where he is."

"And Raden is your other son?" she asked, not wanting to actually look at the man on the ground. She settled for a nod in his general direction.

"My eldest son, and your uncle."

"He tried to kill me, his own niece!" Arica cried in horror.

"You are a threat to him, for it seems the unicorns have named you their True One. I like to think that, in the end, he wouldn't have hurt you. I'm sorry for all he has done to you."

Arica felt a dozen more questions rising to the surface of her mind. She paused. She wanted to sort them in order of importance. "What does True One mean?" she asked.

"You were born with the gift to be one with the unicorns. You share with them, are a part of them and their magic. It happens rarely, perhaps once or twice in a thousand years. You are truthful just as they are. Isn't that right, Arica?"

Arica shrugged. "Lying doesn't make sense. It makes everything worse, even if you don't get caught." But she knew it was more than that.

Grandmother nodded. "The unicorns named you this because they trust you."

Arica wasn't so sure she understood everything Grandmother was getting at, and maybe wouldn't until she'd thought things over. But before she could ask her to explain further, something else popped into her mind.

"One more thing," Arica said uneasily. "It's about Grandfather."

"Ah, yes. Your grandfather. I was wondering when you'd get around to him."

"Is he really dead? I mean . . . lately, I've wondered."

Grandmother laughed, with a sound like the gurgle of water over stones, or the splashing of fish on the surface of a still lake. And with her laughter the tension of the past moments broke, and they all laughed with her.

"Yes . . . and no," Grandmother answered.

Arica stared, hardly believing what Grandmother had just said. This was the same kind of muddled nonsense she had been getting from Grandfather.

But somehow it no longer bothered her so much.

"What do you mean, yes and no?"

"I mean he's not dead, but he's not alive, either. At least, not in the usual sense."

"I think we'd better quit this conversation while we're ahead," Drusa said, putting an arm around Arica's shoulders. Her own shoulders shook with laughter. "You'll learn this about fairies the more you are around them. They always talk in riddles."

"Any more questions?" Grandmother asked.

"Not for now," replied Arica with a sigh. "There's so much to think about. It's making my head hurt."

"I'm going to release your uncle now," Grandmother warned her. "I'll send him away. Don't be afraid. He won't hurt you while I'm here."

Grandmother waved her wand. There was a flash of golden light and Raden, with Arica no longer below him, fell face-first into the dirt. Instantly he was on his feet, glaring at them all, his fists clenched at his sides. The look he sent the unicorns could have shattered a block of ice.

Grandmother spoke in a voice like black clouds and thunder.

"You will no longer make slaves of my elves for profit or put chains on the unicorns. Leave my granddaughter alone or you will have to answer to me. Is that clear?"

For the first time since Arica had known him,

Raden had nothing to say.

Grandmother's voice softened. "It's still not too late, my son. Change your ways. Come back to me. There's always a place for you at my side."

"Is that all, Mother?" he said in a voice like chips of ice on steel.

"I believe it is."

They stood in silence and watched his tall, dark form as it grew smaller and smaller, then slipped behind the rise of a small hill and was gone.

"Come, Arica," said Grandmother, taking her hand. "It's time to go home."

Epilogue

Arica lay in her own clean bed in her own safe room and stared at the small toy unicorn her grandmother had given her for her tenth birthday.

Grandmother had arrived at her party in the middle of the Maurice the Magician act. Shortly afterward, Maurice's ability to make things disappear seemed greatly improved. Later, they ate cake and ice cream and Grandmother placed a small gift wrapped in plain blue paper on the table beside her plate. Then she smiled, looking for all the world like an ordinary, slightly batty, grey-haired grandmother — instead of the Fairy Queen of Bundelag, who silenced evil fairies with a nod and made parents forget their daughter was ever gone.

She had left the party in a great rush, with only a wave goodbye.

The unicorn was made of glass, painted sparkling white, and had dark eyes that seemed to watch her no matter where she went. It could have been Wish standing there on the nightstand beside her bed, crafted of magic and sand. In the dark of her room, the toy unicorn was the only thing that glowed.

A single tear slipped from Arica's eye and fell onto her pillow.

"I miss you, Wish," she said, burying her face in her blankets. "Say you won't forget me. I'll be back some day — Grandmother promised. She said there was something important for me to do in Bundelag, and I know she meant what she said. When that time comes, we'll be together again, and we'll have adventures — though I hope they're not so hard — and we'll go swimming in the river of music, and we'll chase little yellow butterflies through the meadow. Then I'll feed you sour apples till your stomach aches, and you can steal things from my pockets."

Arica sat up to catch her breath, and that's when she heard the bells. They trilled, soft and clear and true — somewhere in that place in her head where she could hear without really hearing, and see and know things better than she could see and know them with her two real eyes.

Then she heard the bells again.

Come soon. I wait, they said.

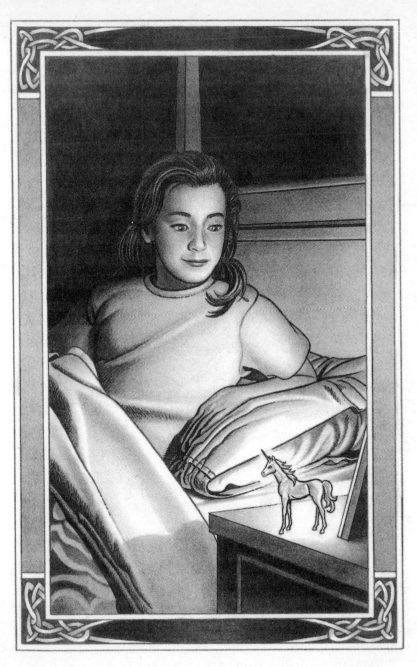

In the dark of her room, the toy unicorn was the only thing that glowed.

Vicki Blum has always loved reading, but as a child she never dreamed she would become a writer. After she was grown up, her brother suggested she try writing books as well as reading them — and a writing career was born.

Vicki lives in High River, Alberta, with her kids and her pet snake. She works with books as an elementary-school librarian, and enjoys doing workshops with young writers. She loves writing fantasy; this is her first book for Scholastic.